T0105893

SAY GOOD-BYE
TO
AUNT CELIA

SAY GOOD-BYE
TO
AUNT CELIA

MAUREEN LYNCH

Order this book online at www.trafford.com
or email orders@trafford.com

Most Trafford titles are also available at major online book retailers.

© Copyright 2012 Maureen Lynch.
All rights reserved. No part of this publication may be reproduced, stored in a
retrieval system, or transmitted, in any form or by any means, electronic, mechanical,
photocopying, recording, or otherwise, without the written prior permission of the author.

Printed in the United States of America.

ISBN: 978-1-4669-1373-8 (sc)
ISBN: 978-1-4669-1372-1 (e)

Trafford rev. 03/30/2012

 www.trafford.com

North America & international
toll-free: 1 888 232 4444 (USA & Canada)
phone: 250 383 6864 ♦ fax: 812 355 4082

SAY GOODBYE TO AUNT CEILA

This twisted tale of a stolen identity will have you spellbound. Melissa, the main character, has only one living relative, an aunt, whom she decides to visit. The trip to Aunt Celia's, in northern Maine, turns out to be a big disappointment. Upon arrival, plans for her aunt's funeral are underway. Melissa has skipped a semester of college to get acquainted with the aunt she has never met; therefore, the news is shocking.

Vera, a college roommate and confidant previously helped Melissa cope with the loss of her parents. Their friendship lasted through the summer by working together in a resort restaurant. Each was fated to meet a love interest that summer, which would last far into the next school year.

Melissa's trip to northern Maine and her aunt's palatial estate entangles a web of intrigue and mystery, which she decides to investigate. Aunt Celia's will can't be read until it is cleared of an extortion charge; therefore, Melissa is required to stay at the mansion until the will is settled.

The employees seem to welcome Melissa to her aunt's home. Larry, the handsome handy man, has a questionable character and a wife that has disappeared. The butler, Sedwig, is a reliable employee whom has worked for Aunt Celia for several years but has a deep, dark, hidden secret. The caretakers, Beverly and Barry, are mainly interested in the aunt's money and do not hide their greed. Their inheritance, from Aunt Celia's will, is the reason they remain at the mansion.

CHAPTER 1

SUMMER AT THE OCEANSIDE RESORT

THE RESORT RESTAURANT in Maine, located on the ocean front, sat tranquil and quiet at the close of business. Melissa and Vera, employed as waitresses, cleaned the kitchen area as instructed on their duty schedule. John, the cook, scrubbed a kitchen grill while whistling along with a tune on a digital touch-screen jukebox. He cleaned up the cook's work area and emptied the fryer grease, into a container, while continually whistling the same tune after the jukebox stopped. He was turning fifty, but had a youthful physique. Only the graying mustache and hair belied his claim of being forty. Paul and Garry, college students, who hoped the summer job, would bring them big bucks made a weak attempt at fulfilling their tasks, which included cleaning sugar bowls, maple syrup pitchers, salt/pepper shakers, and ketchup containers. They were twin brothers with curly blonde hair, blue eyes and a care free attitude about work; probably on pills and stoned most of the time. Melissa and Vera, also college students, eyed the shifty actions of the guys but didn't tattle. The girls wanted to go home after a long hard day on their feet but felt elated as they patted their apron pockets, which budged with tips from happy customers.

"It won't be long before we will be closed for the season," John commented. "In another week it will be Columbus Day Weekend and the work will be over." He wiped his greasy hands, on the soiled white apron, then quickly removed the garment and threw it into a laundry bag.

"I've given my notice. This is my last day," Melissa announced.

The resort restaurant, located on the southern coast of Maine attracted many tourists, to the area, searching for seafood specials and a scenic view of the ocean. A heavy volume of customers required good service, and the patrons showed their appreciation by generous tips. Fresh fish and lobsters are brought in daily by fisherman, boiled in huge pots, baked or fried at the customer's request. The restaurant had an outstanding reputation and attracted customers from around the world.

Melissa and Vera roomed together, in a small apartment, not far from town. Both shared equal expenses; however, had different personalities, which surprisingly seemed to compliment each other. They planned to work at the resort restaurant through the season, but had different itinerancies in the fall. Vera planned to return to college; whereas, Melissa decided to take a semester off to visit her aunt and only living relative.

Melissa had blue eyes, long blonde hair drawn back in a pony tail. Her tall, lanky, sun tan body turned men's heads as she walked by. She was meticulous when it came to make up application using a dark pencil liner to emphasize, the area, around her baby blue eyes, and sparse amount of mascara on the long lashes. Her wide red lips formed a smile, which showed off pearly white teeth in contrast to her dark tan.

Vera was short, stocky and plain looking. She had mousy brown hair, square shaped face, wide nose and sparkling brown eyes. Vera had possibilities of being attractive but chose not to wear makeup to improve her appearance. What she lacked in looks was made up by her sparkling personality. Vera was secretly envious of Melissa because she was the most requested waitress at the restaurant.

Bob, the restaurant manager was in his early twenties and just graduated, from college, with a degree in the Hospitality Field. Impeccable in appearance he dressed in suit and ties, at the restaurant but enjoyed casual attire off duty. The blue eyed manager with light brown stylish hair had a personality that attracted customers. He adored Melissa but the feeling wasn't reciprocated. There was definitely favoritism when work stations were assigned: Melissa always had one fronting the ocean; the most requested seating. Bob hired Vera because Melissa recommended her. When he saw Vera she reminded him of his sister who was outgoing and always said what was on her mind.

Melissa and Vera were college roommates at Worcester State College when the tragedy occurred. Vera consoled her roommate, following the sad news about the tragic plane crash, which took the lives of Melissa's parents on a transatlantic flight from France. Vera's outgoing personality, on campus, made her a popular student so she was able to overshadow the sullen Melissa. No one knew the agony Melissa felt except Vera whom accompanied her to the funeral and stayed by her side during those dark days. The two friends agreed to keep the sad event private. Vera vowed to be Melissa guardian from that time on. They often kept in touch by cell phone.

Melissa inherited the family car, an older model Ford Escort wagon, which was sufficient for trips and economical on gas. The sparse amount of inheritance was gone, after the parent's bills were paid off; therefore, the money leftover barely covered the cost of tuition. There was a law suit, on the airline, which should bring some much needed money to Melissa but it would take time to settle.

"Let's go home," the restaurant manager announced to the crew. "Everything looks clean."

The guys were oblivious to the fact their antics had been observed by the girls.

When they were outside Vera made a remark to them.

"Nice going guys. We saw you hiding the dirty salt shakers and ketchup bottles under the coffee urn instead of filling them. Hope you'll do a better job next time."

"Glad you didn't squeal on us," Garry shouted.

Paul laughed, "Hope no one checks under the coffee urn."

"You guys are awful," Melissa shouted in a disgusted tone.

It had been a long day and both girls wanted to get home and rest; however, the effort was worth the exhaustion: they made an enormous amount of money. Both girls made a mad dash toward the car.

"Guess what?" Vera quizzed as they pulled out of the restaurant parking lot. "I'm going to make my famous spaghetti. This time I'm not getting sauce on the ceiling."

Melissa, whom seemed to be going back into a depression, snapped out of the sad mood. "I'm really going to miss you, Vera. You always say things to make me laugh. I wouldn't have made it through the death of my parents without your help."

"You could come back to college and forget about visiting you Aunt Celia," Vera remarked. "I'm going back late and will have to make up some of my classes."

"No, I really need to meet her. She is my only living relative," Melissa replied.

When they arrived home Vera immediately slipped into the kitchen and started preparing the spaghetti.

The telephone rang.

"I'll get it," Melissa called to Vera. "Oh, hi Bob," Melissa spoke into the mouthpiece. "I can't go out. I'm leaving for northern Maine in the morning. See you next season."

Melissa hung up the phone in an abrupt manner.

Vera poked her head out of the, swinging kitchen, door.

"Leaving poor Bob in the lurch. It's going to break his heart if he has to wait until next year to see you." Vera returned to kitchen duties.

The door bell rang.

"I'll get it," Melissa called to Vera.

Melissa opened the door. A stocky built, bespectacled man, stood frozen, in place, as he held a bouquet of slightly wilted daisies. He regained composure then handed the

flowers to Melissa. She remembered him from the restaurant. Not wanting to hurt his feelings replied. "Oh, Bill you shouldn't have . . . ."

Bill didn't give her time to finish the sentence as he swept past her, in a swift motion, and entered the flat. Melissa was not in the best mood. Her feet ached but she did not want to insult him so she stood, stone still, with a look of dismay. Not knowing what form of action to take. Perhaps she should give him the flowers back and tell him to leave?

Vera peeked out the kitchen door. She thought: What is that guy doing here. She took one look at Melissa's expression and the welted flowers then shook her head. Vera decided it was best not to interfere and returned to the kitchen.

Bill sat down and made himself at home. Melissa was perplexed at the situation.

"Let's go out to dinner. I'm hungry. Where do you want to go?" Bill asked.

"Thank you anyway. Vera is making spaghetti. I have to get up early. I am very tired."

Bill ignored the fact that Melissa was unreceptive. "Do you have a long drive?"

"Yes, it's about 8 hours from here to Station Harbor," Melissa said.

"I guess Vera will be accompanying you?"

"No," Vera said sharply as she exited the kitchen with a bowl of hot spaghetti. "But if that invitation stands, I would love to go out with you Bill. Stay and have some dinner. We can make plans."

Bill got up and darted toward the door. Vera was not as attractive as Melissa and he didn't want to be seen with her; even though he was no beauty.

"That got rid of him," Vera said as Bill slammed the door shut.

Vera let out a belly laugh. "I wouldn't be seen with him, either."

"You mention John, the cook as a romantic interest. Do you still feel that way towards him?" Melissa inquired as she twirled the spaghetti over a spoon and took a mouthful. "This spaghetti is really good."

"Did you notice how intently he looks at me? He asked me out. I think its love," Vera replied.

"Isn't he a bit too old for you?"

"No, I like older men," Vera replied. I know he is, divorced and not good looking but someone that I could hold onto and not worry that he might cheat. I can't wait till college is over. I'm tired of waiting on jerks," Vera continued on another subject. "I worked part-time on week ends, during high school, at this diner, which was hard work and not much money.

"I remember you telling me about that experience. The tips are much better at the resort."

Suddenly both girls became silent as they ate.

"By the way, what's this town like? The place your Aunt Celia lives?" Vera spoke first as she had finished her food. Melissa was still working on a half plate full but started to feel full. They hadn't eaten all day, so both girls, ate most of the spaghetti.

"It's a small town. Population is only one hundred people. Close knit community. Aunt Celia owns a mansion that sits on a cliff overlooking the ocean. She has a male servant, Sedwig, whom has worked there since her husband, Alfred, passed away. Sedwig does odd jobs as well as gardening and daily chores. There is also a maintenance man named Larry. Aunt Celia found him in Augusta when she worked, as a bookkeeper, and Larry moved into the mansion. There is also a married couple, Beverly and Barry, who are caretakers of the property. The estate is huge and a financial burden for Aunt Celia since Alfred died; however, she seems to have enough money and domestic help to maintain the property. I am looking forward to my first visit.

"I hope you will be careful. You don't know anything about your aunt," Vera commented.

Neither girl felt like doing dishes but planned a kitchen clean up in the morning.

"Guess what? Vera queried.

"What? I can't guess."

Vera pulled a chilled bottle of wine, out of the refrigerator, and then offered to pour a glass for Melissa. A can of beer was displayed as an additional choice.

"I prefer wine," Melissa stated.

"I knew you would," Vera said as she popped the cork and poured a glass of wine for Melissa then opened the can of beer for herself. "Good luck to you and a new adventure," she toasted.

"Where will you teach after graduation?" Melissa inquired.

"I'll apply for a teaching position in a school for disabled children. I haven't decided on a particular one. Someday I hope to have children of my own. Hopefully they will be healthy."

A sharp knock on the door startled the two girls. Melissa reluctantly answered it. A handsome young man stood there; for a moment Melissa stood transfixed at the sight. The tall figure had soft doe like brown eyes, which seemed to gaze, at her, in sexual manner transmitting a masculine allure that was hard to ignore. The medium dark blonde hair hid part of his visage. When he brushed it back, there appeared a partially shaven suntanned face. Melissa glanced at his tan, sexy body, which was dressed in cut offs and an old torn-t-shirt. She felt a warm surge.

"Hi! I'm Mark. I live down stairs with my buddies. We're here for the summer. I was wondering if you lovely ladies." He gave Melissa a once over look. "Would like to join us college guys for a drink?"

"If we do," Vera stated. "We can't stay long. I hope no one is drunk."

"No drunker than we are now. I'll give you scouts honor we'll behave. We're three guys from a college in Pennsylvania just having a good time."

Melissa was about to turn down the invitation when Mark leaned against the door and gave her an intense stare, which caused Melissa to blush. There was an attraction that was not to be ignored. Vera immediately recognized the magnetism.

Melissa turned to Vera. "What do you think?"

"If we go, we can't stay long," Vera stated.

The girls left the apartment full of dirty dishes and followed Mark. As he entered the downstairs apartment two guys were hanging out. One fellow was sipping beer and the other smoking bong hits.

"This is Harry and Steve," Mark introduced his friends.

"What's your choice of refreshment?" Mark asked the girls.

"I'll have a beer," Vera requested. Harry gave Vera a wink.

"And you my lovely lady." Mark asked as he lightly brushed her soft blonde hair.

"I don't know," Melissa stuttered. She froze under his touch.

"I'll make you a healthy drink with orange juice," Mark stated.

"That will be fine," Melissa responded.

"You're friend Steve looks high," Vera observed.

Steve was pale, thin and unhealthy looking. His body leaned heavily against the wall to support the frail body. The vacant look, in his eyes, was equivalent to a "do not disturb sign". His stringy, unkempt hair hung over his face and partiality hid the insipid green eyes.

"He does a lot of drugs but is harmless," Harry replied. "It's starting to affect his college grades. Last year he tried coke, hallucinogenic mushrooms and pot. I don't know what he is doing tonight."

"Man I got so high," Steve stammered. "I almost flew out the dorm window one night."

"He's our college roommate. We're very concerned about his future," Mark commented.

The group turned away, from Steve, when they noticed he returned to a lethargic state.

Vera enjoyed conversing with Harry and comparing their college studies, as student teachers, which seemed they had a common interest. Harry was plain looking with dark hair parted in the middle, light blue eyes magnified through horned rimmed eye glasses and a large nose, which seemed to typify his oversized body.

Vera glanced over at Melissa and froze. Mark had her on the sofa and was trying to kiss her. Melissa seemed to be resisting but a bit buzzed.

"That's enough!" Vera shouted. "Let's go."

Vera helped Melissa, off the sofa, awkwardly balancing her then headed toward the door. Harry opened the door and assisted Vera as the ascended the stairway.

"I'm sorry," Mark called after them.

Melissa had a low tolerance to alcohol. Vera helped her up the stairs and entered the apartment with Harry holding Melissa. Melissa staggered toward the bathroom.

Vera thanked Harry. He said good-night and left.

"I guess it wasn't such a good idea to join those guys," Vera stated after Melissa came out of the bathroom and plopped into bed.

"Why not?" Melissa slurred her words. You seem to like Harry."

"We exchanged e-mail addresses and cell phone numbers but I think he has a girlfriend. We do have a lot in common," Vera commented.

"I wish I could stay in touch with Mark," Melissa said as her voice weakened.

"Maybe you can," Vera stated. "Harry and Mark are roommates in college. You need to sleep off the alcohol."

"He is so hot looking," Melissa slurred. "He came real close to being my first love experience," her voice trailed off as she fell into a deep sleep.

"I am so exhausted," Vera spoke low. She went into the living room and made up the sofa bed then collapsed on top.

The morning sunlight woke Vera as she remembered most, of the college, students, had returned to their perspective schools leaving a shortage of help at the restaurant, so it was imperative that she showed up for the breakfast shift. In a week, the restaurant would close for the season. John, the cook, promised to take her out to dinner for the grand finale of the closing then drive her back to the campus. Vera found herself comparing John with Harry. John would always be a cook and would not understand the importance of the profession she chose, a teacher for the learning impaired; whereas, Harry would be a Special Education Teacher. She didn't know much about Harry except the brief conversation where he seemed to share the same hopes and dreams for the future.

Summer attractions were fleeting so she tried to keep the meeting with Harry in the right perspective but promised herself that she would keep in touch with him.

Vera left Melissa asleep in the bedroom and slipped quietly out. She hoped that Melissa's trip to her aunt's would turn out positive and give her some insight into her mother's earlier years.

CHAPTER 2

THE TRIP

SUNSHINE STREAMED THROUGH Melissa's bedroom window and reflected off various objects throughout the room. The intense heat drifted through the window, which caused her to wake in a pool of sweat. The brightness of daylight momentarily blinded her; however, the memories of the previous night seemed to be tucked away, in her mind, as though an effort was made to obliterate them. She had a splitting headache, from the night before, triggered from the alcohol ingested at the social get together. Now she started to piece together remnants of last evening as she reached for an aspirin in the medicine cabinet. The thought of the long drive to Station Harbor, Maine to meet her aunt for the first time filled her with anxiety. Last evening's happenings seemed a bit blurred; however, slowly she started to remember events related to Mark and how he came on to her. The rest was a bit sketchy.

Vera had left for work, which left Melissa, in the flat, void of cheery companionship as she packed for the long trip; therefore, a sense of loneliness encompassed her. To avoid the silence Melissa hummed in a low tone, while clothes were gathered, from the wardrobe, and neatly stacked in the suitcase. She decided on a variety of apparel, which included casual and a few formal dresses. There was always a possibility that an unplanned situation could be in the offing. Did Aunt Celia entertain a lot? Melissa envisioned the atmosphere of a tiny seacoast town in Maine with cool sea breezes, miles of beach and sea water perhaps to dip your feet into but probably too chilly to swim. She was looking forward to delightful chats with her aunt perhaps stories shedding light on her mother's younger years. She glanced at the overstuffed suitcase and decided it was time to secure the big brown valise and get on the road.

Melissa placed the suitcase in the Ford Escort wagon. She stood frozen when a deep masculine voice called out "Hi, how do you feel this morning? She turned and saw Mark. Once again confronted with a strange feeling, at the sound of Mark's voice, warm sparks flowed through her body.

"I just wanted to apologize. Your friend told me I was out of order." Mark said in a warm apologetic voice.

"She is overly protective," Melissa explained.

"Would you e-mail or cell phone me?" She didn't know how to reply. Mark handed her a slip of paper. "By the way, I would like to leave you with one parting gesture."

Mark gently placed his arms around Melissa's shoulders then planted a light kiss on her lips. She was taken aback by his action but melted at Mark's touch. He released her, opened the vehicle door, and assisted her as she maneuvered into the driver's seat. As she drove away the temptation to glance into the rear view mirror overtook her better judgement because it reflected Mark's image watching her departure. Soon the image grew fainter and fainter as she drove farther away. An empty feeling came over her when the realization hit that Mark was gone, at least, for the time being.

Melissa drove north toward the nearest turnpike exit. She drove through an interesting stretch of winding road bordering Route 1. A large selection of motels, restaurants and shops; various advertisement for special rates were posted to attract tourist. She slowed down, as she entered a town, which hosted a variety of famous actors, in season, at the Ogunquit Playhouse. The summer season had ended but early fall is a beautiful time of the year. The leaves, on the trees, were changing color: tourists swarm the area to see the spectacular multicolor fall show.

Melissa forgot that she hadn't eaten anything but her stomach churned as a reminder so she stopped, at a restaurant, to have breakfast before picking up the interstate. Melissa spotted a small cafe, with few cars, and then pulled into the parking lot. The interior, of the dining room, was dotted with autographed posters of stars who had performed at the Ogunquit Playhouse, which was an interesting touch for the eatery. The service turned out to be superb. There were only two tables occupied throughout the exquisite eatery. Both tables had couples in deep conversation as they ate a hearty breakfast. The waitress approached Melissa's table holding a coffee pot in one hand and an order pad in the other.

"You must've read my mind, Sally," Melissa read the waitress's nametag then turned the cup over so Sally could pour the hot coffee.

pulled over to the side and parked so she could eat. Melissa glanced around while she relaxed and sipped the coke. Across the street were a row of the structures, which had been recently built and reflected modern age engineering skills. As she glanced further down the street a reflection of the past caught her eye. Three workmen on a high bucket lift supported by a crane repaired a church steeple. The structure seemed to be in ill repair; however, it represented architecture of a past era.

The brief respite seemed to energize her body, which started to feel the affects of the night before; therefore, she needed to reach Aunt Celia's house before exhaustion set in. Melissa traveled for a couple of hours before entering a secondary road, which was on an oceanfront. A sign read 'Welcome to Winter Harbor'. She gave a sigh of relief since the point of destination was only another hour. The sunlight slowly dimmed; however, Melissa put the car sun visor down to shield the late afternoon rays, which reflected off the water. The ocean fronted Winter Harbor and would guide her, scenic route, all the way to Station Harbor. Every now and then she glanced over at the sparking waves floating toward the shore. The observation included people laughing as they frolicked in the water and ran through the sand seemingly oblivious to the chilly temperatures.

Melissa opened the driver's side window, which allowed a seaweed/fish smell into the vehicle. A gentle ocean breeze caught her hair and blew it in an upsweep but she didn't care because the cold air brought her into an alert state, which she needed to navigate the winding road. She traveled for an hour before the scenery changed. The ocean no longer fronted the road instead its angry foamy waves hit against the rising cliffs, along the ocean front, which Aunt Celia described in a letter. A row of homes, sporadically located, stood on high receding cliffs: in the vicinity was an old lighthouse.

It was in this locality Aunt Celia's house, a three story, mansion was located.

Melissa stopped the vehicle in an area, which seemed to fit the description. A sign post confirmed, CELIA'S ESTATE NO TRESPASSERS ALLOWED that it belonged to her aunt. This was it! Melissa heart started to pound as she sat frozen but recovered when a car horned, in back, indicating she was blocking the road. She waved them by. She glanced down the cliff, to the oceanfront and noticed a yacht attached to a dock area. The yacht swayed to a fro as it pulled away from the mooring. It must be part of Aunt Celia's estate she surmised.

Melissa pulled into the driveway, of the mansion, which had a long and fairly steep incline. In the rear, of the mansion, gardens bloomed still arrayed with a variety of flowers and a lovely sweet aroma filled the air. Melissa reasoned, with well kept landscape and garden, Aunt Celia had employed a top notched gardener. Parking, on a precipice, was not easy and she followed the signs to the visitor's parking area then put on the emergency brake.

She walked unsteadily to the front door, glanced around, making an observation, of the enormous estate; wondered how Aunt Celia could afford to keep it up. Her body felt cramped due to amount of time spent in the car without stretching. She pressed the doorbell. It rang loudly and echoed inside the mansion. A very solemn man appeared at the door. Melissa surmised it must be Sedwig.

"I'm Melissa Johnson. Aunt Celia is expecting me. I'm her niece."

Melissa observed a tiny built man with a thin wisp of white hair neatly combed back. Sedwig was dressed in black. His face was round but wrinkled and pale with a zombie like appearance. Even his actions seemed automated. The small dark eyes peered out of hollow grooves. The butler bowed his head as he spoke.

"Come in Miss Johnson. I assume you came for Ms. Celia's funeral."

"She died?"

"Yes, I'm afraid so. Her wake is tomorrow. She did indicate that you will be included in the will. Her lawyer will be glad that you came," Sedwig said expressionless as he motioned Melissa inside.

Melissa stood in the entry hall in a state of shock. She observed Sedwig and remembered Aunt Celia's praise of his faithful service after Uncle Alfred died. His appearance and actions were a bit scary but, she surmised, it was because of his age.

"I will bring your luggage inside. Your room is on the second floor. No one, with the exception of the cats Sylvie and Simon, are allowed on the third floor. When she was alive it was Ms. Celia's private area. I hope you will respect her wishes." Melissa nodded in agreement then handed Sedwig the car keys so he could retrieve her luggage.

Melissa stood alone and quietly observed the interior of Aunt Celia's mansion. The floors, in the front entry hall, were made of marble. The lovely mahogany side table, which supported a Ming vase with intricate designs painted on the surface, showed off some colorful, fresh, fragrant roses. A crystal chandelier hung above. Melissa's second glance, viewed several other antique lighting fixtures, which led into the front room. She had a sneak peek into the interior and noticed Aunt Celia loved paintings, expensive furniture and draperies. The sleek designer furniture, yellow/ red tones, matched the plush rug.

Sedwig came inside with the luggage and motioned Melissa to follow him up the mahogany, well polished, wooden stairs with a red runner carpet that was a bit frayed. The room Sedwig entered was adorned with an oriental rug. Tapestries hung on the walls. The red velvet draperies matched the bed comforter. It didn't seem homey: too many luxuries.

"This is your room," Sedwig announced. "Dinner is served promptly at 6:00. There will be other guests arriving to attend the wake." He left her alone.

It was such an empty feeling and a disappointment. She came all the way here to be with her only living relative. Now her aunt was dead. Sedwig was a cold person. No use asking him about Aunt Celia. If only Vera was here. She could confide in her. Who were the guests and the other members of the household? She would soon find out.

There was a knock on the door.

"Who is there?" Melissa questioned.

"It's Beverly. I was a close friend of your Aunt's. I'm so sorry for your loss."

Melissa opened the door and viewed middle aged women. She was well built, in her fifties and smartly dressed. Her snow white hair was neatly pulled tightly in a pug, which gave a clear view, of her face. The well tanned woman had a perfect oval shaped face, with warm brown eyes, and an elongated nose. Perhaps a former beauty queen at some time in her life and now kept the image through face lifts: Melissa surmised.

"You must come down for dinner soon. I want you to meet my husband Barry."

"I guess I won't have time to take a nap," Melissa said. "I feel tired but I can have dinner first." Beverly departed. Melissa took her time to bath and dress. The stressful day finally caught up as she lay down on the red velvet comforter and napped; therefore, an hour had past before she descended the elegant staircase and was ushered into the dining room by a well tanned, middle aged gentleman waiting for her at the foot of the stairs. He took her hand and he re-entered the dining room. She assumed it was Barry.

Sedwig gave her a hard look as he spoke.

"Dinner is served promptly at 6:00 not 6:10. His voice was cold as he spoke. The look of distain sent chills down her spine.

Beverly rose from the table. "This is Barry. He is so gracious."

Barry bowed, at the introduction, and motioned to Melissa to sit as he pulled a chair away from the table. She sat and he gently situated the chair in a comfortable position. He then took a seat next to Beverly.

The first impression of Barry, a middle aged, well groomed, and impeccably dressed man with a young physique was positive. His bushy white haired framed his square face and the glasses, which he wore loosely on the broad nose, seemed to enhance the dark brown eyes.

Melissa glanced over, to the opposite side of the table, where a strange young man sat. She judged his age to be somewhere in the thirties. Melissa noticed the deep tan, blonde hair, and blue eyes, which radiated a certain sexual appeal. The wide grim seemed to welcome her but he didn't fit in with the rest of the household. He wore an old T-shirt and jeans, which seemed out of place with the rest of the guest who were dressed in stylish attire.

Beverly noticed the bewildered look.

"Larry is the handy man around here. We need him for maintenance jobs," Beverly explained. "Barry and I are the caretakers of the property."

Melissa nodded in his direction. Larry gave a friendly waving gesture in return.

She still wondered why he was at the dinner table.

A young girl exited, from the kitchen. Her wide almond shaped brown eyes, dark skin and lovely face glowed with beauty. The smile showed beautiful white teeth. The dark hair was tied up in a red bandana. The aroma emanating from the soup she ladled into the bowls had a special effect on one's gastric juices.

"Jesse is from Boston." She graduated from a famous cooking school. Her family came from the Caribbean, first settled in Boston then here. Your aunt hired her and she has been such an asset to the household. Don't you agree she is a fabulous cook?" Beverly said as she sipped the crème of broccoli soup. Jesse had returned to the kitchen and did not hear the compliment.

"Yes, it's full of culinary delights," Melissa agreed.

"We only have healthy meals here," Barry added.

The household members were quiet during the rest of the meal being served; perhaps it was the long table that discouraged conversation. Cloth napkins, which were a silky texture and matched the tablecloth. In the middle sat a lovely water crystal ornament, with several bowls jetting out on the side, which ensured each had their own finger bowl. Beverly sat opposite on Barry at the elongated table. Melissa took a sneak peek, at Larry, now and then as he dropped a morsel, on the lovely blue/red silky tablecloth, then roughly wiped his face on a cloth napkin. Melissa pretended not to notice his crude manners; however, it was hard to ignore since she sat directly across. The sparkling crystal glasses and bone china dinnerware caught her attention; therefore, she concentrated on the elegance, which surrounded them. The cats ran, to and fro, under the table scouting for scraps of food. Sylvie, the female cat seemed to like Melissa as she brushed up against her leg in a loving manner. Melissa cautiously, reached under the table, and dropped a tiny piece of chicken and hoped no one noticed. Sedwig was not in the room. Larry grinned slyly at Melissa, a knowing gesture, but it was a guarded action shielded from Barry's and Beverly's view. He cautiously looked away when Jesse came to serve the desserts.

The silence was broken as Beverly spoke. "Tomorrow is the wake. Only one service will be necessary."

"When is the funeral? I didn't come prepared. I don't have anything black to wear," Melissa spoke in a whiney voice.

"No funeral. The casket will be closed. The body is to be cremated. The wake is informal so black attire is not necessary. A luncheon is to follow," Beverly informed.

"Is there a reason for the closed coffin?" Melissa asked. She so wanted to see her aunt. Then it dawned on her, perhaps her aunt had a disease and the procedure was necessary.

"It's better that no one knows the answer," Beverly replied. That silenced Melissa.

Beverly and Barry Mosley invited Melissa to join them in an after dinner cocktail but she decided against consuming more alcohol because of her low tolerance to the spirits. Vera was not present to assist her if she felt dizzy. They couple proceeded into the drawing room where the bar was located.

"Come this way," a voice ushered. "I'll show you around." Larry led her into the library, which had an extensive selection of literary books, magazines and newspapers. A computer sat on an antique desk with a matching chair. Not far from this area was a red velvet sofa and chair situated adjacent to an unlit fireplace. Some unique paintings hung on the mahogany paneled wall.

Melissa followed Larry down a narrow passageway as continued the tour, of the house, then stopped at a closed door.

"This is a room used for business by, Mr. Clark, your aunt's lawyer. He keeps all the paperwork pertaining to the estate and Celia's will. I guess he will be arriving for the wake. We keep this room locked," Larry advised her.

They continued down the passageway and stopped at a glassed in sunroom. The sun shone brightly, through the solar panels, and showered the rays on an array of plants, which dotted the interior of the room with a variety of colors.

There was a dark corner, of the house, further down the passageway; however, he quickly summoned her to follow him away from that area. They quickly walked back into the main house and entered the living room where Larry lit a fire, in the oversized fireplace and bade her to recline in one of the comfortable chairs. It seemed warm and cozy after the fire caught. Larry went to a corner cabinet and poured a sherry. Melissa hesitated to take the drink then surmised one glass, of sherry, wouldn't make her drunk. Larry placed the glass on the side mahogany table next to a vase of fresh flowers and Melissa relaxed. Larry sat, on the plush yellow/red sofa and raised his sherry glass.

"To Celia," he toasted.

"Aunt Celia has very good taste. The house is exquisite." Melissa observed.

"She left us a lot of money," Larry added.

"I wish I could've known her," Melissa sobbed.

"Don't be sad," Larry said as he handed her a tissue to wipe the tears. "She was a wonderful, happy, and generous person. We can sit by the fire and enjoy our drink. That's what she wanted."

Melissa nodded in agreement as she sipped the sherry and hoped, a little alcohol, wouldn't make her tipsy. Vera wasn't here to help. Not much was said after the discussion. Melissa offered to take the empty glasses to the kitchen when they were finished.

"OK," Larry agreed. "I have to check with Beverly about tomorrow's work schedule. See you tomorrow."

Melissa had the impression that Beverly was in charge of the house now that Celia was gone. Was she the procurator of the will?

Melissa entered the kitchen. Jessie was busy rinsing the dishes and placing them in the dishwasher. Jessie turned toward Melissa and in a low tone said, "If I was you I wouldn't stay here."

"What did you say?" Melissa wasn't sure if she heard right.

"Watch your back while you are here," Jessie whispered.

Sedwig entered, the kitchen, and Jessie became silent.

"You need to get your work done and leave," Sedwig ordered.

Melissa quickly exited the kitchen but felt a bit uneasy about the warning Jessie had given. She said good-night to Larry, Beverly and Barry. Larry held a piece of paper as the three discussed a plan of action. Melissa assumed it was for some repair work.

Melissa made her way up the stairs. It would be good to have a restful sleep; therefore, she quickly changed into a nightgown, pulled the comforter back, and then froze as a set of footsteps shuffled in the hall. She peeked out the bedroom door, which was only slightly opened and viewed Larry, as he proceeded to climb the stairs to the third floor. A key turned in the lock and a creaky door opened then shut. Thank goodness Larry hadn't noticed her. The footsteps above made Melissa aware that some activity, perhaps a repair job, was taking place. She silently left the room and glanced up the third floor landing, Simeon, the male cat stared back at her from above. The stripped yellow/brown tiger cat had large brown eyes that glowed in the dark. He curled up near the closed door and looked up at it as if he wanted someone to let him inside. Melissa crept back to her bedroom, slipped into bed and fell asleep.

Melissa woke and glanced at the bedside clock, which indicated it was only 2:00 AM. She heard footsteps as someone descended the steps, from the third floor, and decided it was not wise to open the bedroom door at this hour. Suddenly the downstairs door opened and closed. Curiosity got the better of her so she glanced out the window to get a glimpse. The moonlight gave her a good view of Larry. What was he doing at this hour in the morning? He was digging something up, near the gazebo, and then putting papers in a bag. It looked, as though, a box was filled with some type of papers but she couldn't tell exactly at this distance. Larry stuffed some, of the papers; in his pocket then reburied the container along the side of the gazebo replaced a plant over the freshly dug soil. As he returned to the house, with the bag, she backed away from the window.

CHAPTER 3

THE WAKE

THE TOWN'S PASTOR, Reverend Stanley, stood by the door greeting friends, family, and business associates of Aunt Celia's as they arrived at the funeral parlor for a short prayer service. The reverend was an elderly man, wrinkled visage with narrow brown eyes that crinkled up as he smiled. Some of the townspeople gathered at Celia's casket to pay their condolences as the reverend stood nearby tightly, clutching a prayer book, with trembling hands. He walked toward the podium with an unsteady gait to set up the program. The service was delayed for an unexpected guest. Someone whispered, in the back, the reverend may be afflicted with Parkinson's disease; however, it could be old age. Nevertheless, he was to officiate over the funeral service, which would be nontraditional and done according to the instructions Celia left. Her remains will be cremated and ashes spread into the ocean immediately after the prayer service.

"When the cremation has been completed people are invited to gather, on the boat dock, to witness the spread of Celia's ashes out to sea," the Reverend explained with a quivering voice.

Melissa glanced around the small funeral parlor. The funeral director, a very close friend of her aunt's, came over and started introducing Melissa to several of the town's business people. The postmaster, the grocery clerk, the drug store pharmacist, banker, baker and friends were all pleased to meet a blood relative of Celia's. She had been so gracious and generous to the whole town that Melissa was treated as royalty. More people poured into the room and passed by the closed coffin to pay their respects. A picture of Celia's younger years was affixed to the outside, of the coffin, so people could cherish her memory. The group took their seats to prepare for the reverend's sermon. It was so crowded, in the parlor, that Melissa couldn't breathe. Someone opened a few windows before the service.

The reverend stopped his eulogy, in the middle of a sentence, and glanced up as a stranger limped into the room; pivoting on a cane to maintain his balance. His face twisted in pain as he walked. Someone got up to assist and guide him to a chair.

"It's Alfred's brother, Leo, whom arrived at the service. Leo stayed by Celia's side after, her husband, Alfred died. Poor man had been in a bad auto accident now he lives off social security and on a run down farm. He didn't do as well as Alfred so there was friction between the brothers. When Alfred was alive Leo tried to borrow large sums of money to pay off bills. I think Celia gave Leo a substantial amount to help out after Alfred's death. "That's Nellie!" Melissa viewed a young girl, in her twenties, short cropped hair, overweight, expressionless and dressed in overalls. Nellie assisted Leo but seemed to have a bad attitude about the burdensome task. Leo limped as he walked, being burdened with an arthritic condition, which seemed to have progressed. His white hair was unkempt, and leathery skin obliterated the small eyes. One suspender, on his overalls, came loose. Both Leo and Nellie paid their respects, in front of the closed coffin, and then quickly took seats. The town's gossip monger whispered to Melissa. "Nellie is a relative of Leo's and a nurse's aide. She takes care of him."

Melissa thought it was her fate to encounter gabby people. The woman stopped talking as the reverend continued the eulogy, then paused, and invited people to come forth with praises of Celia. A long line formed and one by one they approached the front, of the room, to sing praises of Celia with different stories regarding her financial assistance in difficult times. Melissa sat back proud of her aunt's accomplishments.

After the service, Melissa followed Beverly toward the closed coffin. They knelt, on a soft cushioned board, in front of the coffin and paid their last respects. Melissa glanced, at the picture attached to the coffin, and noticed how young her aunt looked. Beverly reminded Melissa about the luncheon by pointing to her watch. They silently left the funeral parlor. As they walked toward the church hall Melissa questioned Beverly about her aunt's different appearance. Pictures her mother had given her did not resemble her aunt as depicted on the coffin.

"Celia had a lot of plastic surgery. It changed her appearance. She convinced me to go to her doctor. He's in Europe and does a fantastic job," Beverly stated.

Melissa assumed that something went wrong with her aunt's plastic surgery; maybe that was why the casket was closed. The only visual memory, of her aunt, was the picture on the closed coffin. She didn't want to imagine anything else.

Reverend Stanley welcomed people as they entered the church hall cafeteria where the luncheon was set-up. He cheerfully greeted the guest and invited them to join the festive luncheon. A happening Celia had planned before her death. The next event, the group was reminded of, was a short ceremony where Celia's ashes would be scattered into the sea. "You should be proud," the reverend addressed Melissa as she entered. "Your aunt was a pillar of the community." Melissa smiled proudly.

"The service was brief," Melissa remarked to Beverly as they stood in the buffet line.

"It was done according to your aunt's wishes," Beverly replied.

The aroma was a gastric delight. Jesse, her mother and sisters were in the kitchen portion of the church hall. Larry was up front spooning a variety of eats; his plate overflowing. He tried to balance a drink as he walked slowly toward a long banquet table where Sedwig and Barry were seated. Just as he reached the table, his drink tumbled onto the floor. Luckily, the spill was quickly contained. The two men ignored Larry's clumsiness as they were affixed on devouring their food.

As Melissa passed through the buffet line, carefully selecting a variety of eats, she noticed Jesse's hard stare emanating from the kitchen. It sent chills down her spine. It was unnerving. Jesse was warning about something but she couldn't quite grasp the full meaning so Melissa disregarded the girl's stare: perhaps she was jealous.

Melissa joined the other household members at the bench style banquet table. She tried to get the incident out of her mind and concentrate on the meal. The food was so good that several people were going back for seconds. It probably wasn't the proper time to discuss anything tragic; however, Melissa casual inquired about the time of the cremation ceremony.

Beverly had a morsel, of food, in her mouth and hesitated before she answered. "Celia's ashes will be back from the crematory about 5:00. The Reverend will say a blessing then scatter the ashes into the ocean. We will meet at the boat dock about 5:15. She continued to eat and became silent. After the luncheon, Beverly went into the kitchen to discuss dinner plans with Jesse and her family. She stayed there helping with kitchen clean up.

"I think Beverly is instructing Jesse to save the buffet's leftovers for later; therefore, no one will have to cook an evening meal. I don't mind. The food is delicious," Larry commented as he stuffed another portion into his mouth. He talked as he ate. Grouse! Melissa thought.

Larry finished the large portion of food then pushed the empty plate to the far end of the table. "Guess this is enough until later," he said as he got up to leave. "Beverly is preoccupied, in the kitchen, so I'll walk you back to mansion."

Melissa followed Larry, past several buffet tables, where people were still enjoying their lunch and discussing future town plans. One group stopped talking to acknowledge the departure of Melissa and Larry. One woman said, "We'll see you at the dock for the distribution of Celia's ashes."

The oceanfront path, designated for walkers, led them past large homes and mansions, which fronted the walkway. "Look down the cliff!" Larry instructed as he pointed in a downward gesture. Melissa gazed down the steep incline and saw a stone ladder built into the cliff, which led to a boat dock. "There is where the scattering of Celia's remains will take place." Larry commented. "I don't know who she left the yacht to. I hope it was me? I'll take you out on the yacht. I'm a licensed boat pilot."

Melissa wondered how she would fare descending the ladder. There was a secure hand rail to hold onto. It still looked like a fairly steep drop; however, to honor her aunt's memory she would do anything; Melissa wasn't looking forward to the feat. Larry seemed more interested in money than sad about Celia's passing. He wanted to take Melissa out on the yacht? She had never been on one before.

Seagulls, high above, circled the two as they walked and seemed to signal a warning with their loud cries.

They reached Celia's mansion and Larry ushered her inside. Sedwig was still at the church hall so they stood alone, in the entry hall; facing each other, possibly a magnetic attraction occurred between them. Melissa was aware of Larry's uncanny activities so she guarded against any romantic feelings.

At first neither spoke then Larry broke the silence, "I could stand a glass of sherry. How about you?"

"Yes, I'll have a glass, too."

Larry placed his arm lightly around her shoulders as they walked into the living room. Melissa reclined, on the loveseat, while Larry poured the sherry.

"Here's to Celia! The lawyer will be here to read the will tonight!" Larry raised the sherry glass to toast.

Melissa joined in the toast. She brushed away tears from her eyes.

"I have a few maintenance jobs to do so I'll have to leave you after we partake of this delectable glass of sherry," Larry sat close to her on the loveseat then shifted to a chair when the front door opened.

Melissa remembered the early morning episode. Larry was digging something up. Was it part of his chores? At 2:00 in the morning. There must be a logical explanation she convinced herself and kept silent about the whole incident.

Larry left her alone in the living room. Sedwig had returned and was busy arranging the coat closet; therefore, Melissa was able to slip out the door without being noticed. She roamed around the estate admiring the enormous layout. Statues, of goddesses, dotted the garden area and picturesque water fountains flowed through the mouth's of dragons and bubbled in a soothing tone. Around the back was a tennis court. Adjacent to the court was a small cottage probably a servant's residence. She circled the estate and came back toward the gazebo. A fresh mound of grass had been dug up, soil replaced, and a plant inserted over the area. Perhaps it would be dangerous to know, what was under the soil, buried in a box. As Melissa looked toward the house she noticed

Larry's face peering out a window. He was watching her explore? The sun was bright but a chill was in the air so she returned to the mansion.

Melissa ventured toward the library and selected a poetry book, which was part of a collection, then decided to get her coat and go outside. Even the slight chill outside would be a welcome relief to the dark and damp mansion.

Larry was repairing the door. "Nice day to sit at the gazebo and read," he said.

"Yes, I've selected a book on romantic poetry," Melissa responded.

"Enjoy!" he said with a wide smile then turned back to the repair job.

Melissa sauntered over to the gazebo and up the three stairs, which led to the interior. The entwined top was made of weather treated bamboo, as were the sides; however, a special type of wood re-enforced the enclosure on all angles. She had her choice of seating and viewing. She chose the left, which had a lovely view of the gardens, and a partial glimpse of the sea. The gazebo's circular bench would allow one to sit and absorb the enormous beauty of nature. There was an aroma of garden flowers still in bloom. Two peacocks roamed around the gazebo, one had a plain brown feather span, while the second displayed a beautiful radiant colored plumage. As they strutted, around the garden, Melissa observed their actions as well as other birds that used the bird bath and feeders. A Blue Jay and Cardinal flew by, and then ascended on the bronze embossed bird feeder. Sparrows searched for food on the ground, while a dove, cooed in a nearby oak tree.

This is heaven Melissa thought! She started reading the poetry book and was lost in its contents until a car came into the driveway. It was Beverly and Barry returning from the church hall. They carried in trays and boxes from the buffet luncheon. Sedwig and Larry brought carts out then wheeled cases of soda, from the car, into the kitchen area. Melissa decided she would assist in some way; however, by the time she got to the car everything was inside.

An after thought occurred to Melissa. Sedwig would be angry if she was late for dinner so not chancing an awkward situation went inside and peeked into the kitchen. Sedwig was warming some leftovers, looked up with a blank expression. There was nothing in his body language that she could detect; therefore, she took the book and went into the sunroom to finish reading the contents. Perhaps Sedwig was upset about Celia's passing?

"We help ourselves to leftovers in the kitchen tonight," Larry informed her as he entered the sunroom. He unfastened the tool belt, attached to his waist, and placed it on a table in the sunroom. "Let's go! We need to eat before the ceremony! "We don't want to miss Celia's distribution of ashes," Larry stated.

Melissa went toward the library to replace the poetry book and noticed family members as they walked by the room, in a trance, and headed toward the kitchen. She replaced the book, then followed Beverly into the kitchen and mechanically replicated her actions as she picked up a plate, napkin and silverware. A variety of warmed buffet items in a steam table emanated a savory aroma. Beverly exited the kitchen with a variety of eats on her plate. Melissa undecided looked over the cold cut and salad selection. Larry was busily spooning food into a plate. "I think the food is better warmed over," he remarked. He quickly left the kitchen to join the others. Melissa still debated on what to eat. She was full from lunch; therefore, selected a small salad from the buffet. Melissa grasped the dinner plate and a fruit drink, and then joined the other members of the household at the dining room table. A solemn silence fell over everyone as they ate. The entire group was sad at the loss except Larry, nothing could upset his appetite.

After dinner, Celia's household members and staff gathered at the rugged stairway leading down to the dock area where the ceremony was to take place. Reverend Stanley had to be helped down the jagged stairway ladder, which was a feat at his age. His hair blew in the wind and his fragile body maneuvered slowly down ladder. Barry descended behind him and was ready to catch the Reverend if he lost balance. Cautiously, the others, close friends and the only blood relative, Melissa, made their way down to the dock area. The Reverend requested silence and a lowering of heads as he said a prayer over Celia's remains. When the crowd looked up the Reverend opened the urn, and then sporadically distributed Celia's ashes into the sea using a golden ladle. The ceremony was over in ten minutes. Melissa dreaded the climb up; however, Larry assisted her and it took less time for her to reach the precipice than anticipated.

Tom and Nellie stood on the upper portion, of the cliff, and viewed the ceremony from above. It was too difficult, in Tom's condition, to climb down the steep embankment. They gave Melissa a hug when she reached the top. Larry stood there assisting others as they climbed toward the top of the ladder.

Seagulls circled around anticipating tidbits of food.

Melissa engaged a conversation with Tom and Nellie. "I didn't realize Aunt Celia had relatives."

"Well, we did what we could," Tom commented. "Celia had a heavy burden to carry after my brother Alfred died. Celia was busy bookkeeping in Augusta. We hardly saw her. She had to work to keep this estate up. We tried to get her to sell but she wouldn't."

"You couldn't blame her. It's so beautiful," Nellie said as she glanced up at the mansion.

Beverly was the last person up the ladder. She turned toward the Reverend and thanked him for the lovely service then invited him to a cocktail hour at the mansion; however, he declined due to a previous commitment. Some of the other townspeople decided to accept and followed Beverly back to the mansion where Barry had set up a bar. Sedwig placed snacks, on the kitchen counter, for the guests and disappeared with a drink to soothe his nerves. After all these years of service it was hard to adjust.

Larry walked back to the mansion with Melissa. Rotating beams, emanating from the lighthouse, led the way. Tom and Nellie trailed behind due to his injury and inability to walk fast.

Melissa could hear Tom whisper to Nellie, "I hope Celia left us something in her will."

Larry spoke low to Melissa, "We will soon find out. Mr. Clark will be here tonight. Let's head for the library and have a sherry. I don't like crowds. When they entered, the mansion, Larry gently took her arm and they went toward the library where he gallantly led Melissa to a comfortable chair, lit the fireplace, then went over to the miniature bar and poured two glasses of sherry.

Sedwig came into the library. "I need a drink," he stated.

"I though you didn't drink? Larry inquired. "Help yourself."

"I need something to get me through their stay. Tom and Nellie drive me crazy with all their requests. Get me this. Get me that," Sedwig said as he downed the glass of sherry and poured another.

"Oh, there you are," Nellie said as she peeked into the library. "Tom needs some more snacks. We are about to run out." Nellie quickly left.

"You see what I mean," Sedwig said.

The look of dismay on Sedwig's face was the first emotion displayed by him. Sedwig jumped up, from the chair, as the melodic sound of doorbell chimes echoed throughout the mansion. "That would be Mr. Clark, the lawyer, I presume," Sedwig stated. "I hope I don't look drunk." He stood there and straightened his tie and attire before proceeding toward the front door.

"We'll, have to finish up our glass of sherry and join the others in the study. Cocktail hour is over and guests have departed. I think Mr. Clark came to read the will," Larry informed. He took Melissa's hand and pulled her out of the sunken chair and onto an upright position. She had been so comfortable, in the library, that the thought of being led into the study where the antique chairs were hard seemed a punishment; however, she followed and took a seat next to Larry.

Mr. Clark stood in front of a mahogany desk strewn with paperwork. The bald headed, oversized man was clean shaven. The egg shaped face accented the wide smile, which seemed phony; however, didn't hide the discolored teeth, which was a result of too much smoking. He winked at Melissa, then widely opened his big brown eyes to view the group assembled for the reading of the will. The exquisite suit, he wore, was tailored to fit his body. It was brown tweed with a matching shirt and tie.

The lawyer spoke to the gathering. "I'm Walter Clark. I'm here to settle Celia's will but unfortunately there has been a postponement due to allegations of embezzlement, lodged against Celia by a former employer. The theft occurred when she worked in Augusta as a bookkeeper; therefore, she has been included as a suspect along with other employees. The auditors will be here tomorrow to go over the estate's books; however, I am going to legally restrict them from some of her personal documents. As far as I'm concerned the company does not have concrete evidence that Celia was involved in any of this, so they will have to prove the charges." Mr. Clark collected the papers, on the desk, and put them into his briefcase.

Melissa was dismayed at the accusation against her aunt. Although she hadn't met her Melissa doubted the serious charge and was upset that anyone dared muddy her name. There were whispers throughout the room.

"I want complete co-operation when the auditors arrive tomorrow. I will need the study unoccupied during their stay. I hope this matter will be resolved quickly so we can settle the will." Mr. Clark secured his briefcase and followed Beverly to a private area for a discussion on the company's legal rights to examine Celia's paperwork, auditor's arrival, and arrangements. A separate downstairs area would be reserved for their stay.

"I was wonderin how she could afford expensive things while we struggled to make ends meet," Tom said sarcastically.

"Hush!" Nellie said. She gave Tom a disgusted look. "Don't accuse Celia before the facts are known. Now come along. You're going to take a nap. We have connecting rooms on the left wing of the first floor. If you need anything just call." Nellie assisted Tom as they slowly exited the study.

Walter Clark stood pensively studying a document then glanced up to see Melissa standing alone in the room. She seemed perplexed about the situation and questioned, "What proof did the company have to accuse Aunt Celia of a theft?"

"There is an ongoing investigation," Walter answered. "Celia seemed to be the victim of identity theft. It appeared an unknown woman used her credit cards, which occurred before her death. I have been working with credit investigators and the police to uncover the one responsible. That's all I can tell you for now," Walter said. He looked admiringly, at Melissa. You sure are an attractive young lady. Too bad Celia didn't live to see you." Then he became absorb in a pile of paperwork, which discouraged any further discussion.

"Goodnight I'm a bit tired," she commented mostly to herself.

"I'll be here all night straightening the files for the auditors arrival tomorrow," Walter commented lost in though as he shuffled through the massive pile of papers. I hope Beverly will keep the coffee on. She allowed Sedwig to go to the servants quarters so he could rest for the busy day tomorrow."

It was early morning when Melissa woke. It was pitch dark outside. She rolled over and tried to go back to sleep but the nagging thoughts about her aunt's name being rolled in the mud bothered her. Perhaps she could go downstairs and get a cup of coffee.

Melissa made her way down the staircase. Walter's loud voice came booming through the study door. Then a weaker feminine voice could be heard. It was probably Beverly helping Walter as he straightened out the files. Melissa walked on tip-toes toward the kitchen, to get coffee, and tried not to disturb them.

Walter's voice became louder, "We're going to alter some of these receipts. Then a weak voice spoke low. Walter answered, "Yes, they will be checking everything. They don't have definite proof that anything is amiss because there were other clerks in the office that are under suspicion. We still don't know who the woman is but Celia's credit cards have been used as far away as Florida.

"I'll be assisting you in adjusting Celia's books," Beverly stated in a higher pitched tone than previously used. "We have to cover up certain aspects of her death."

Melissa gulped the coffee down and cautiously crept upstairs so no one would detect her presence. The conversation seemed strange. She heard Beverly say Aunt Celia's books should be adjusted and something to do with a cover up? Cover up Celia's death?

Melissa quietly climbed back into bed but couldn't sleep and laid there wondering who would steal Aunt Celia's identity. Suddenly, she heard a shuffling of feet above, on the third floor, and nervously rolled over and buried her head in the pillow. The sound stopped as quickly as it started. Melissa fell back to sleep.

Melissa woke about 6:00 in the morning with the sun partially streaming through the velvet red drapes. A smell of fresh made coffee drifted all the way upstairs so she quickly dressed and made her way to the kitchen. Sedwig was brewing a gourmet blend, which had an aroma of hazelnut. She walked by the study and noticed it was vacant so she entered the room, then closed the door so she wouldn't be detected. Melissa started shuffling through a stack of charge receipts, taking notes on items spent and places where they were purchased. A few of Aunt Celia's personal documents and receipts were scattered, on the desk top; however, others were placed in neat rows. One receipt was a charge at The Shady Palms Motel in Augusta. It sounded seedy. Why would she want to stay there? Melissa quickly annotated the name, date and time on a pad. Some of the signatures, on various charges, didn't match with others. There were other suspicious transactions in Augusta. There were charge receipts from Florida, New York, Philadelphia and Georgia. Among receipts of interest was an address of an apartment house in Florida, which she jotted down. She was determined to find the woman whom took on Aunt Celia's identity.

A shadowy figure entered the room. Melissa jumped.

"I seen you look through that stack of papers," Tom said. Melissa turned to view Tom as he struggled to walk with his cane.

"You won't say anything, will you?" Melissa begged.

"No, I think something funny is going on, also. I'm just too sick to look into it," Tom allowed Melissa to help him to the front room then into a comfortable chair.

"Where is Nellie?"

"I think she is sleeping late," Tom replied.

Sedwig entered the front room. "I have fresh Danish and hot coffee," he stated.

"I'll get you a tray. Just sit there and relax," Melissa addressed Tom. She went into the kitchen to fix a tray. When Melissa returned Nellie was standing, in the middle of the front room, yawning. Melissa handed her the tray with coffee and a Danish roll aware that Tom could not handle the hot coffee. Nellie would know best how to assist Tom.

"We're headin for home. Get yourself some grub. We have chores at home.

When all this malarkey is over we'll return for the readin of the will," Tom said to Nellie.

Melissa returned to the kitchen and sat on a high stool. Sedwig came over with a hot Danish roll, offered on a decorative Dresden plate, and then poured her coffee. She was taken aback at his kind action. Maybe he was growing fond of her, after all? Nellie came in grabbed a Danish and swiftly swallowed a cup of coffee.

"We're leaving," she informed Sedwig. "Thank Beverly for her hospitality." Nellie totally ignored Melissa.

"Do you need assistance with your luggage?" Sedwig queried.

"Na, I can carry them," Nellie remarked. She left the kitchen. There were loud footsteps, in the entry hall, and then the front door slammed shut.

"They don't act like part of our family," Sedwig remarked to Melissa.

Walter entered the kitchen. He grabbed a coffee with his Danish roll. He nodded to Melissa and Sedwig as he passed through the kitchen on his way to the study. Beverly came into the room with Barry trailing behind. "It's not going to be a good day. Best stay out of the auditors' way," Beverly commented to Melissa. The couple poured coffee and were off for a run.

Melissa went into the library and selected a book then headed toward the sunroom to read. Larry came into the room and re-attached the tool belt around his waist.

"I have some repairs to do around here then you and I are going fishing," he announced. "The auditors have arrived and are in the study with Walter. The door is closed."

"I would love to go out and get some fresh ocean air," Melissa stated.

"Later, then," Larry waved.

Melissa was half way through, the second book in a poetry series, when Larry appeared at the sunroom door. He took off the tool belt and set it on the sunroom table.

"Let's go! We can grab some finger sandwiches Sedwig made for lunch and a couple of sodas," Larry remarked.

"How are we going to get the food down the steep stairway?"

"I have a special devise strapped on that can carry various items. So don't worry. Here is your fishing rod," Larry handed her a small rod. I have the bait and tackles. Sedwig handed him a package, which Larry inserted into one of the many pockets of the contraction hooked onto his body. They left the mansion, crossed the street: Melissa, once again, looked down at the steep drop: dreading descending the ladder.

"I'll go first. Don't look down. I'll be right behind you," he reassured.

Cautiously Melissa made her way down the rugged stone ladder grasping the side handle for secure support. Larry slowly descended the ladder behind her. When they had reached the wharf he baited the fishing poles and they sat dangling them in the cool water. The breeze caught Melissa hair and blew it wildly about her face.

Larry reached into his pouch contraption and pulled out a sweater, which he placed around Melissa's shoulders to keep her warm.

"I didn't realize it would be so chilly here," she remarked.

"It's always breezy by the water especially this time of year. Lucky for you I was thinking ahead. When you are hungry let me know. We can sit on the beach and eat." Larry said.

"Do you really think Aunt Celia embezzled money from that company?" Melissa asked.

"No, I don't. She was the sweetest, kindest, most generous person," Larry responded. "Don't worry! They won't prove anything."

Melissa seemed satisfied with that answer. A sudden tug on her line indicated she had caught a fish. Larry reeled it in for her. It was a catfish.

"Better than nothing," Larry laughed. "I haven't caught a thing." He released the fish and threw it back into the ocean.

"Have you ever married?" Melissa stumbled over the words.

"Ya, I was married when I lived in August but we never had kids. I'm divorced now. I met Celia shortly after the divorce. She advertised in the Augusta paper for a maintenance man. Never thought I'd live in a mansion on the seacoast at that time but she needed someone to make repairs. The house is old and it's a constant upkeep.

So here I am! Enough chatter about me. Let's take the yacht out."

"Are you sure it will be alright?" Melissa was a bit leery.

"Sure! Celia always allowed me to captain the yacht. I even brought a hat with a brim," Larry said as he pulled a crumbled hat, out of the contraption, with many compartments. "We can have our finger sandwiches and sodas as we cruise by the shore."

"I hope 1 don't get seasick," Melissa stated as Larry helped her onto the rocking vessel. Its plush interior was quite like the inside, of the mansion, with numerous red velvet furnishing. A bar sat in the middle. Plush red velvet recliners, anchored firmly, circled the bar it as if readied for a party. The pilot's area was shielded by a curtain and not visible from the interior. The deck had a shiny white texture, which seemed slippery.

"We have a small restaurant at our disposal," Larry said as he pulled a devise from the wall, which housed a stove and microwave. I won't show you downstairs yet. There are two rooms, one master bedroom and a smaller room. You sit tight and I'll start the engine. Place it on automatic pilot so we can have our lunch and sightsee. I'll leave the sandwiches and sodas here."

Melissa wondered why Larry had all these privileges. It seemed strange for a handy man to have so many luxuries at his disposal. She relaxed, in plush red velvet chair then placed the sandwich and soda on an anchored side table.

The yacht started smoothly then slowly cruised around the overhanging cliffs and beautiful homes atop them. They ate in silence, and then Larry started naming the various property owners and Celia's relationship to them. It would turn out to be a short tour just to introduce Melissa to the town and their inhabitants. They returned to the dock mooring.

Larry caught Melissa, in his arms, as she slid on the slippery deck. "You are very attractive," he commented as he brushed the blonde hair away from her face.

"You're a lot older than I am," Melissa retorted sharply.

"Physical age doesn't matter. It's appearance and the way you act," Larry responded then released his hold on Melissa.

She brushed the whole incident off as a fluke and hoped there would be no recurrence. Larry helped her climb back onto the precipice and they both headed toward the mansion. Larry's mood became distant. It was close to 6:00 dinner time. He left Melissa and rushed inside for dinner. The auditor's cars were no longer in their respective parking area. They had departed for the day.

Melissa didn't have time to change and hoped no one would notice her jogging suit as she entered the dining room. Larry was already seated. Beverly and Barry had solemn faces as they waited for Jesse to serve the meal.

"I am glad you are on time," Sedwig commented, to Melissa, as he passed through the dining room. He seemed to be warming up to her.

Jesse served a scrumptious three course meal. Melissa didn't look up as an uneasy feeling enveloped her when she faced Jesse. Jesse wanted to convey some information but what?

After dinner, Melissa followed Larry into the library. Exhaustion started to set into her body from a very active day. Larry seemed tired also and when he poured their glasses of sherry he slowly lifted the glass and stated. "This is to toast Celia and her innocence. The news is they haven't found any evidence!" Then he quickly lowered the glass and drank the contents with one swift gulp, sat down and fell asleep.

Melissa took the two dirty glasses into the kitchen. Jesse stood, at the sink, rinsing dishes before placing them in the dishwasher. She looked up and made a quick comment, "If I was you I'd stay away from Larry. He's trouble."

Sedwig entered the kitchen. "Are your chores finished?" He questioned Jesse.

"Almost," she replied.

Melissa left swiftly and retreated to her bedroom. Another warning? Jesse was telling her something but she couldn't quite grasp the message. Was Jesse jealous of Larry? She had another restless night. Sylvie, the cat, curled up on the bed next to her. The grey/black stripped, green eyed bundle of fur was the only comfort she had.

TRIP TO AUGUSTA

FALL ARRIVED, USHERING into the region bitter cold temperatures that reached below freezing. Certain varieties of trees shed their leaves, and were at the mercy of the weather as bare branches exposed to the elements formed ice on their bark. Harsh breezes picked up the fallen leaves, as the wind heightened they were caught up in an upward motion, and flew through the air until the gale abated. The multi-colorful leaves formed miniature tornadoes, which encircled the gazebo and made it an unsafe harbor as the cold breeze whipped through the partial enclosure. Most birds took flight, while others sought refuge at a bird sanctuary on the grounds.

Melissa was caught in a gigantic wind tunnel as she walked outside to view the enormity of the waves pounding the shore. High waves swept wildly over the dock area where the yacht was tied up and caused it to rock, back and forth, pulling away from the mooring. Only a huge rope, tied to a steel bar, anchored the yacht. A huge ocean storm had arrived. Her hair blew unrestrained as the wind caught her and whipped open the thin jacket. The sea moisture soaked her clothing as she struggled against the wind to return to the mansion.

Seagulls were carried away by the wind as they tried to reach a secure area of land. Their unsettled cries were eerie.

Sedwig stood, in the kitchen, pensively gazing outside. "The weather is frightful," he commented as Melissa entered the back door. "You need to get dry and I'll bring you hot tea in the sunroom. Take that wet jacket off."

Melissa instinctively obeyed and handed the jacket to Sedwig. He, in turn, gave her a kitchen towel to soak up the moisture. She went upstairs and changed the drenched clothing. Was Sedwig starting to like her? He seemed a bit kinder. She went downstairs and waited in the sunroom for the hot tea. Soon Sedwig appeared with refreshments.

The glass enclosure, in the sunroom, gave off solar heat and a clear view of the storm as broken tree limb pieces, sand, and other debris flew by and hit the windows.

Melissa reclined in one of the rattan chairs, covered with a blanket, and sipped hot tea. When she felt comfortably warm it was time to explore the forbidden area, which was dark. She was surprised to find nothing taboo was there. It had a computer and a copy machine. Great! She thought. I can e-mail Vera and invite her for the holidays.

Larry had taken one of Celia's vehicles to a garage, for a tune up, so he wouldn't be around. It was quiet almost eerie in the mansion. Melissa finished the e-mail and went back into the sunroom to admire the interior. It was a gardener's delight with all the colorful plants and flowers. The heavenly aroma of various flowers filled her nostrils.

"You like flowers?" Beverly glanced into the sunroom. "I keep them watered and fed with special plant food then watch as the sun does the rest.

"Yes, the fragrant aroma and colorful contrast, of the arrangements, are so professionally done," Melissa replied.

Then she changed the subject. "By the way, I plan to go shopping in Augusta tomorrow. I need some warm clothes."

"Be careful driving. I hear we are getting a small dusting of snow," Beverly cautioned. At least you'll get away from the auditors. Those guys make me nervous. I'll be glad when it's all over."

Dinner was quiet. Sedwig served the meal stating that Jesse was not feeling well. Neither Jesse nor Larry was present. Was that food for thought?

Early the next morning Melissa left for Augusta. The sky was grey and threatening but the wind had died down. Now there was a threat of snow. The windshield wipers moved in a repetitive motion wiping the sleet/rain mixture from front window as the car drove away from the mansion. The drive was long and tedious; however, the traffic was sparse because of the hazardous road conditions. Upon entering, a suburb of the city, Melissa viewed a "Welcome to Augusta" signpost. She hadn't eaten and craved a cup of coffee; therefore, she maneuvered the car into a restaurant parking lot located in the outskirts of the city. When the car engine was turned off the squeaky windshield wiper's noise ceased, which was a relief. The repetitive noise had gotten on her nerves the entire trip.

Melissa entered the restaurant and selected a window seat where she could gaze outside and admire the scenery.

A cow pasture, coated lightly with snow, hosted a row of green pine trees laden with a white hue, which sparkled in the dim daylight. The scene reminded her of Christmas past and artificial snow she threw on a newly cut fragrant pine tree her parent's selected for that occasion. The presents were plentiful under the tree. Now only memories of them remain.

A familiar voice brought her back into reality. "We meet again," Sally said as she poured hot coffee in Melissa's cup. "What brings you to Augusta?"

"Mainly shopping," Melissa replied.

"I'm off in half an hour. I can show you around town," Sally offered.

"Sounds like a good idea. There are a couple of places I'd like to find but I'm not sure of the location," Melissa replied. "I'll have the breakfast sandwich special while I wait."

Sally circled around the room serving other customer's coffee then disappeared into the kitchen. Within a short period of time she approached Melissa's table with the breakfast sandwich and a refill of coffee.

"I'm bushed. I've been on my feet all day," Sally said as she poured the coffee refill into Melissa cup. "Why don't you leave your car here and we can go around in my car?"

"That's a great idea since I don't know the area. Do you know where Shady Pine Motel is located?" Melissa questioned.

"I think I do but I'll check with the cook. He is from Augusta so he will know the location for sure," Sally replied.

"I have a favor to ask," Melissa approached the request rather slowly. "When we get to the motel, can you go in alone and asked the desk clerk who stayed in room 308 on," Melissa checked the charge receipt. "June 3rd and used the name Smith. Try to get the description. My boyfriend is seeing someone else and I'm trying to get the low down on him."

"Sounds like a James Bond assignment but I'll do it," Sally joked.

Melissa ate breakfast and sipped the coffee while Sally finished her shift.

"We have a stroke of good luck." Sally addressed Melissa as she removed her waitress apron. "Charlie, the cook, knew where this motel is located. Just two miles down the road. Let's go," Sally was ready to leave and Melissa followed. Sally's car was an older model Ford Taurus but started as soon as she turned the key in the ignition. Her car wipers moved fast and cleared most the moisture off the front window. It was cold; however, soon the heater took the chill away and it was comfortable inside the vehicle. The sleet had turned to rain and it was quite apparent it was going to be a bad weather day. Sally loaded some food containers into the back seat, which released an aromatic odor throughout the vehicle.

Sally drove two miles, and then turned into a motel, where the signpost was slightly hidden from the busy highway. The old but clear lettered guidepost, indicated they had arrived at the Shady Pines Motel, where Sally followed a red arrow, which directed them to the main office. The main motel area was nestled between several pine trees and had cabins, for rent, in the rear. Sally went inside to question the room clerk. The wait seemed long to Melissa and hoped Sally hadn't run into any problems.

Finally, Sally returned to the car and started chatting. "I charmed the clerk. At first he was reluctant to give me any information but I convinced him that I was relative and new in town so I was looking for my brother. I told the clerk my brother was in protective custody because he was going to testify against a gangster and was going under an assumed name. The clerk looked at me rather strange. Anyway, I wore him down with my gift to gab so he finally gave me some solid facts. Seems like your boyfriend, Mr. Smith, is it? Anyways he was here with a lady friend. She was dressed rather strange. She wore a black veil over her face and a long black dress. It's anyone guess who the lady is. The guy had sandy blonde hair, muscular and a nice tan. Does that sound like your guy? The clerk was really glad to get rid of me."

"Yes, it describes Larry. Can you do me another favor? I have a home address. I'd like you to knock on this person's door and describe the individual who answers. I'll check the name on the mail box because I'm looking for a certain person. You can pretend to be selling some type of item. OK." Melissa requested.

"It's a tall order but I'll do it," Sally said.

Sally drove to a duplex apartment where Melissa checked two different mail boxes. A name, on one mail box, matched the name on the charge receipt. There were actually two names scribbled on the paper. One was her aunt's and the other person lived in portion B of this building. Bertha Sanderson was inscribed on the box.

"Just ask for Bertha. The last name seems familiar," Melissa remarked.

"Could it be your boyfriend is married?" Sally queried.

"That is where I heard it before. It's Larry's last name Melissa," whispered.

Melissa watched from the car as Sally rang the bell. A petite woman answered the door. Sally was gabbing a mile a minute. They chatted for about ten minutes then she returned to the car.

"I was right. Your boyfriend has a wife. The woman who answered the door was named Mille. She said that Bertha used to live there. I think they were friends because I got a lot of information about the whereabouts of Bertha. She moved to Florida. I even got her address. Seems like Bertha is lying low in Florida waiting for a rich old lady to die and leave her money. Hope you can find another guy. This one is real bad news. I have to get back to the apartment to feed mom. I have some stew the cook gave me. The reason I came back to Augusta is that my mother is elderly. My sister took care of her for awhile until she was diagnosed with cancer.

Melissa secretly wanted to return to the restaurant and get her car; however, Sally had been so co-operative in getting the information needed that she felt obligated.

Now she knew who stole Aunt Celia's identity. It was Larry's wife. Were they involved in a scheme? Did they kill her aunt?

Sally sped away from the building and traveled two miles before maneuvering, her vehicle, into a parking lot adjacent to a run down apartment. It had several units. Melissa followed Sally down a long hall past several doors with apartment numbers. When they reach #8 Sally stopped, knocked twice, and inserted a key into the lock. It was a signal she was home.

They stepped into the sparsely furnished front room.

"I still haven't bought much furniture. Just a few odds and ends," Sally commented. "Mom I'm home. I brought company."

A few minutes later a tiny, frail, elderly women walked slowly into the front room. She had wavy white hair, which hung uncombed over her wrinkled face. As she moved toward a chair she clutched the robe with one thin boney hand. The other hand held a cane, which supported her unsteady movements.

"Ma, how are you feeling? You shouldn't have gotten up." Sally gently scolded her. "This is Melissa. Melissa this is my mother. She is Sally 1 and I'm Sally 2."

Melissa softly touched the frail extended hand of the elderly lady. "I am so glad to meet you."

The mother's voice was barely audible but Melissa recognized, by her gesture, Sally's mother acknowledged the greeting.

"Well, now that the introductions are over time to eat," Sally stated. Sally took a pot, from the cupboard, and started warming the stew then opened the second bag, which contained a variety of finger sandwiches. They were displayed on a make shift table along with dishes and utensils.

Sally's mother reclined, in a chair, beside a small side table and waited for her daughter to assist her. Melissa looked around the apartment, which was a far cry from the mansion. The kitchen was small and almost situated in the front room.

Melissa took a small portion of stew and savored the taste; however, secretly she wished to be on her way but didn't want to seem impolite. She had to be patient while Sally fed her mother before she could get a ride to the restaurant.

"My I use your bathroom?" Melissa asked.

"Straight down the hall. It's the room on the left," Sally stated as she concentrated on the mother's food intake.

Melissa walked down the long hall. She glanced, into the two bedrooms, which were situated adjacent to each other. One was neatly kept while the other had a lot of clutter. She guessed Sally kept her mother's room immaculate.

Melissa returned to the front room and noticed the mother moved the spoonful of stew away as Sally tried to serve her more.

"I guess she has had enough," Sally remarked. "I'll help her back to bed then give you a ride to the restaurant."

"Nice to meet you," the mother feebly remark to Melissa as she allowed Sally to assist her in an unsteadily walk.

"It's been a pleasure," Melissa replied as she watched as Sally took her mother, by the arm, and helped her down the long hall toward the bedroom.

Not much conversation between the two as Sally drove Melissa back to the restaurant. Sally seemed deeply worried. It was unusual for her to be so silent; however, her mother's condition looked terminal.

"I don't think my mother will be around much longer," Sally commented as she drove into the restaurant parking lot, and pulled up next to the Ford Escort Wagon. "Hope you find another boyfriend. I think this one is married."

Melissa was anxious to go back to the mansion but she had to shop for some warm clothes. She turned to address Sally before brushing the light layer of snow off the car.

"Thank you for helping uncovering this guy's deception. I think this trip to Augusta answered my doubts. Now I'm on my way to a shopping spree to heal my broken heart," Melissa said as she waved to Sally.

Sally blurted out, "If you need anymore help you know where to find me." She waved as the vehicle sped out of the parking lot.

Melissa cleaned the snow off her car and proceeded to the nearest shopping mall. There were a multitude of stores, which lined the huge complex. She got out of the car and viewed various shops and their techniques to attract customers. Some forms, of advertisement, were 50% off sales and others a big discount if you applied for a charge card. One window display, in particular, caught her interest because of the youthful styles on the mannequins. It sealed her decision on where to shop.

Melissa entered the store. Light camisoles in various colors with matching sweaters were displayed on the upper wall. Designer jeans manufacturer made with rips and patches caught her eye; however, she needed to dress as elegantly to fit in with the group. She remembered that Larry dressed down but he was accepted in the category of a maintenance man.

More would be expected of her since she was Aunt Celia's niece. She focused on a group of pantsuit, which could be worn on any occasion. Her mind shifted to Larry and how he avoided telling her he was still married. What was he digging up? Why wasn't the casket open? Her mind wondered away from shopping and onto the happenings at the mansion.

A voice startled her, "May I help you?" A sales clerk stood in back of the clothes rack. Melissa turned and faced her. The nametag, lettered Mrs. James, hung loosely over her black cashmere sweater.

Mrs. James had an elegant figure, tall, stately and thin. The black skirt with the cashmere sweater gave her a fashion model aura. Her soft brown hazel eyes came clearly into view after she removed the eye glasses, which she clasped lightly between her fingers. They seemed to move with every gesture she made with her hand. Her round face seemed to have a forced smile put on for customers. The hair-do was so perfect that Melissa suspected that the saleslady wore a dark wig.

Would a middle age clerk understand what a young college student was looking for? Melissa was questioning this in her mind as she looked around for a younger clerk but did not see any. It was the middle of the week and most of them would be in school.

"May I help you?" Mrs. James repeated. Her head held high in a superior manner. "These junior coats just came in," she continued. Before Melissa could say anything the clerk took a coat off the rack and held it out so she could try it on. To her amazement, it fit perfectly. She decided to buy it. Then Mrs. James, a crafty sales lady, suggested other outfits that would go together. Melissa was in an out of the dressing room. She started to like Mrs. James suggestions and soon had an armful of items, which was quickly transferred to a hand carried basket. Realizing it was getting late she thanked Mrs. James for the assistance, made a brief stop at the jewelry counter where she purchased a floral sterling necklace with matching earrings for Beverly.

Melissa looked at the time. It was after 6 and she would miss dinner. People started to crowd into the mall, probably the evening shoppers so she quickly paid for the clothes at the main register and exited the building rushing past several milling customers. She neatly placed the bags in the passenger's seat while she cleared the light dusting of snow off the car and quickly drove out of the mall and toward Station Harbor. It was getting dark and the road was slippery. The windshield wipers were not working properly.

Melissa cautiously moved in the direction of the road, which would take her to Station Harbor. Her car lights gave out a steady bean and assisted her in navigating safely on the highway. Then suddenly the squeaky windshield wipers came apart and she was unable to see the road as the blinding snow accumulated on the front window. The situation was dire as the vehicle spun out of control and swung off the highway. She closed her eyes briefly until the car came to an abrupt stop then opened them. A tree had blocked the flow of travel. Luckily she did not get hurt but the car had a big dent on the passenger's side. A passing motorist stopped to help.

"I'll call the State Police," the concerned man stated. "Are you alright? I can call an ambulance also."

Before Melissa could object he used his cell phone to dial the police.

"I think I'm alright. My car may needs to be pulled out. It has a big dent in the side. I can't drive it home. The windshield wipers came apart and caused the accident."

Melissa noted the man was well dressed for the weather. He wore a lightweight goose down jacket loosely fitted around his body with an attached hood. His face seemed hidden with the hood tightly drawn over his face. She would never know his identity; however, always remember him as Good Samaritan. He was there when she needed assistance; then disappeared as soon as the police arrived.

A State Policeman was on the scene in a few minutes.

"I'm Sgt. Joe Holloway," he introduced himself. "Are you hurt?" Melissa nodded in a negative gesture. "I have to write an accident report." Joe Holloway pulled out a pad of paper and pencil. "We'll fill out the report in the police car." He motioned to Melissa to get inside the police car where it was warm.

Joe Holloway was very handsome in his uniform Melissa thought. Tall and muscular and polite but the shiny wedding ban on his finger indicated he was taken.

Joe radioed for a tow truck then got inside, the police car, and asked Melissa a few questions regarding the accident. Slippery road conditions and the faulty windshield wiper were blamed for the accident. Within minutes the tow truck had arrived.

"The tow truck driver will give you a ride home and tow your vehicle. If you need any help with your insurance company give me a call. He handed her his card.," Joe tipped his hat as a parting gesture. His dark skin showed off the big brown eyes and sandy blonde hair. A big smile showed off his handsome face.

The tow truck driver pulled Melissa's car, out of a huge snow bank, and was hitching the vehicle, behind the truck, with steel cables so it would stay in place.

"Come on, lady. What's your address?" The tow truck driver asked as he opened the truck door to let her in and helped her step up into the cab with bundles of sale purchases.

"I live in Station Harbor," Melissa blurted out. She was still chilled and frightened from the accident.

The tow truck pulled out onto the highway. The police car followed a short distance then turned around and headed back to Augusta.

Bill was the driver's name. His green work shirt had it embroidered on a pocket. He was a middle aged, ruddy faced man whose hands appeared calloused from hard work. The road conditions were dire and he concentrated on keeping the car, in tow. He kept a safe distance from other vehicles. He was quiet all the way to Station Harbor until he pulled into the driveway of Celia's estate.

"You live in one of these ritzy neighborhoods," he commented. Then went in back and unhooked her vehicle.

Melissa was still trembling from the accident. She handed him her credit card to pay for the tow but ignored his comment.

"Maybe you should have a doctor look at you," he said in a parting comment.

The tow truck pulled away. Melissa entered the house with her packages and faced a stern Sedwig.

"Where have you been? You missed dinner," he scolded her.

"I was in an auto mishap. The car skidded off the road. I'm a bit shook up. I had the car towed. It's badly dented," Melissa sobbed.

"Go upstairs and take a hot bath. I'll fix you a snack and hot tea," Sedwig's voice softened.

"No, thank you. I just need some time to relax," Melissa said.

Melissa went upstairs. She ached all over. Maybe a hot bath would do her good? Melissa painfully maneuvered her way upstairs to the bedroom, where she undressed, took a hot bath, then laid down on the red velvet bedspread and fell asleep.

She awoke early morning with hunger pangs. The kitchen would be empty and she could get a snack. Melissa descended the stairs cautiously feeling stiff all over from the accident. She crept along the sideboard, in the hall, making way into the kitchen trying not to be detected. Loud voices emanating from the study were Mr. Clark's and Larry's in a heated discussion.

"The Shady Pine Motel Clerk called," Mr. Clark said. "The clerk claimed a woman was nosing around asking questions about you."

"Did he get a good look at the women?" Larry's voice was low keyed.

"Yes, she was middle aged. Said she was a relative of yours," Mr. Clark retorted.

"I don't have any relatives in this area. Was anyone with her?" Larry questioned.

"There was another woman in the car but the clerk couldn't describe her at that distance," Mr. Clark informed. He didn't get a license plate either."

"That's not a good sign. Someone may be on to us," Larry sounded worried.

"Well, it's your neck," Mr. Clark stated. "I have to go now. My wife will wonder what happened to me."

The front door opened then closed. Mr. Clark had departed.

Larry startled her as he entered the kitchen. Melissa jumped and dropped the milk carton she had opened.

"You seem nervous tonight," Larry said.

"Yes, it's was the accident. I'm still shaky," Melissa replied.

"I hope you didn't get hurt," His voiced softened.

"No, but my car is badly damaged."

"I'll get it towed to the body shop tomorrow," Larry offered.

Melissa noticed Larry's dirt embedded jeans but tried not to be too obvious.

"That would be good," she replied.

"Good night." He gave her a friendly salute then went upstairs.

Melissa quickly ate a cookie with glass of milk for a chaser. That should satisfy her hunger until breakfast. The house was silent and dark. She ascended the stairway to her room. Above, on the third floor, there were footsteps. Her whole body felt sore. A state of exhaustion had set-in, so she fell into bed and a deep sleep. She was glad Larry didn't suspect her of snooping.

Chapter 5

VERA VISITS

NOVEMBER'S CHILLY BREEZE filled the air; however, plans for Thanksgiving overshadowed the cold, dark days, which occurred in late fall. The sound of holiday music echoed throughout the mansion infusing holiday cheer into the environment. Jesse, her mother and sisters worked in the kitchen preparing gourmet dishes. The aroma of fresh baked sweets permeated the air and sent out gastric invitations to all who breathe the scent.

"It's the way Celia would have wanted the holidays to be celebrated. They meant so much to her," Beverly explained.

"I have invited a guest to spend the Thanksgiving Holidays here. I hope that was alright?" Melissa said coyly. She forgot to ask permission.

"We have plenty of room," Beverly replied cheerfully. "There is another spare bedroom, upstairs, just down the hall from your room."

Melissa gave a sighed of relief. She didn't want to upset Beverly. The jewelry purchased for Beverly, in Augusta, would serve as a thank you on Christmas Day.

Beverly faded into the kitchen to supervise the activities.

Melissa sauntered toward the library mentally concentrating on what to read. As she passed the study, a heavy puff of smoke filled her nostrils. One glance, into the room, identified Mr. Clark as the perpetrator of foul air. The fat man, oblivious to his surroundings, was puffing on a huge cigar as he thumbed through some paperwork on the desk. He didn't look up as Melissa coughed so she quickened her pace to avoid the toxic air. The library had a wide variety of literary material; therefore, her selection was given to the mood of the day, which turned out to be a suspense novel. Being immersed in the story would serve as a temporary haven to all the worries, which plagued her emotionally. She still had aches and pains from the accident and had no idea how much money the car repairs would cost or when the vehicle would be fixed. Vera could give her a ride, if needed, and she desperately wanted to confide in someone about the strange happenings but her cell phone did not work so she couldn't contact her.

The sunroom was filled with blinding sunlight, which reflected off the glass solar panels that encircled the room. White snowflakes trickled down and integrated into the various snow banks. The weight of the snow caused some tree limbs to bend downward. Melissa rolled down a couple of bamboo shades and pulled up a rattan chair, to a section of the room, which was shaded and seemed most acceptable for reading. Her nostrils breathe in the fragrant scent of the flowers, which surrounded the sunroom. She curled up, in the elongated chair, and then started to read. Suddenly, a loud banging sound interrupted her concentration on the story she was reading. It caused Melissa to jump up, put the novel down and try to identify the source of interference but after checking she found nothing unusual. Probably Larry, she surmised, doing repair work. Melissa tried to block out any additional sounds and concentrate on the rest of the story; however, she was unable to finish the book.

Melissa received an e-mail from Vera, which stated she would arrive the beginning of Thanksgiving week. Vera's family had a vacation home in Florida and they would be away for awhile. School schedule would not allow enough time, at Thanksgiving, for her to go to Florida and spend that holiday with them; instead she would spend Christmas vacation in Florida. Vera was elated to receive Melissa's invitation for Thanksgiving week.

Melissa sprang, out of bed, and glanced at the clock. The bright sunshine, streamed through the bedroom windows, and reflected off a glass framed picture, which hanging on the wall. She overslept and remembered Vera would travel, in the morning, to avoid early darkness of November days. It was her first trip to Station Harbor and with the curvaceous highway it would be easier to maneuver in daylight and find the mansion. Melissa dressed and tidied up her bedroom then went downstairs.

"You're finally up," Sedwig scolded her. "I hope the coffee isn't cold."

Melissa was getting used to his zombie like appearance. His attitude toward her changed daily and she started to ignore his snide remarks.

"Yes," she replied. "A friend will arrive today to spend a few days."

Beverly burst into the room. "We finally have good news on the audit," she cheerfully acknowledged. "The auditors are almost finished and haven't found anything suspicious in Celia's paperwork; however, they do know someone stole her identity and possibly that person was responsible for thefts, which occurred at the company. They still haven't identified the person. Anyway, it seems her name will be cleared. Perhaps in the next month the reading of her will. The auditors are taking Thanksgiving week off but they will be back. I am so tired of them," Beverly voice dropped from excitement to distain.

"That means I'll probably be leaving soon," Melissa conjured.

"Nonsense! Stay here as long as you like. Barry and I plan to buy a condo in Florida after everything is settled," Beverly informed. "But I'm sure Celia would want you to stay awhile."

At first Melissa thought that Beverly might be the person whom stole Aunt Celia's identity but enlightened when proof arose that Larry's wife probably used Aunt Celia's credit cards.

Beverly made a fresh pot of coffee then offered a cup to Melissa. They sat down at the kitchen nook. Sedwig brought some toast with fresh Maine blueberry jam and placed it on the table. Melissa wanted to disclose the discovery of Larry's wife; however, Beverly picked up a newspaper and seemed to concentrate on the news. This was a signal perhaps it wasn't the right time. When Barry entered Beverly put down the paper and started bragging about her weight loss. Barry had a coffee and instant breakfast then encouraged Beverly to join him for a run around the perimeter of the estate.

Beverly said to Melissa, "Have a nice day. I hope your friend arrives soon. The spare bedroom is prepared for her." The couple went off on a fitness run.

Melissa went to the library selected a new adventure book to read then off to the sunroom where she could relax; however, other matters entered her mind and she couldn't focus on the story. When would Vera get here? She needed to confide in someone.

"Good morning," Sedwig's voice greeted from afar. "Come inside. We have been expecting you."

Melissa returned the book; she was reading, to its original place and darted down the hall.

Vera viewed Melissa and rushed over to give her a friendly hug.

"Can I take your suitcase to your room?" Sedwig offered. "Dinner is served promptly at six."

Vera stood in awe at the elaborately decor in the interior of the mansion. She didn't answer.

"That would be very nice," Melissa spoke. "After, could you bring us a pot of coffee in the sunroom?"

"Very well," Sedwig replied, then pick up the suitcase and disappeared upstairs.

Melissa took her friend, by the arm, and guided her toward the sunroom.

"I want you to see where I spend my days reading," Melissa said.

"The whole house is so elegant. I had no idea you were living in the lap of luxury," Vera commented as she glanced aimlessly from one area to another.

They entered the sunroom where the sunshine emanated warmth and glow, which was rare to encounter this time of the year.

"What a beautiful aroma. It's like walking in garden of fragrant flowers," Vera stated as she made an effort, to name each plant.

"Well, what have we here?" a masculine voice spoke. Larry came into the sunroom.

"Vera, this is Larry, the handy man. He does repairs in the mansion."

Vera nodded her head in acknowledgement.

Larry didn't take much interest in the plain looking Vera. "I have some repair work to do. I'll leave you girls alone," Larry said as he exited the room.

"What a hunk," Vera commented. "I just bet you're in love with him."

"You don't know the half of it. I can't tell you here. We need to go out and have breakfast so I can explain." Melissa stopped talking as Sedwig entered the room with a coffee pot, placing a colorful cloth on the glass coffee table, and then pouring coffee in the bone china cups. He handed Vera the first cup of coffee then Melissa next, bowed and left the room.

"I hope I don't break anything," Vera commented to Melissa. "You know how clumsy I am. Now what is this about?"

"Someone stole Aunt Celia's identity. She was accused of embezzling company funds. They've had auditors here looking through her books. Until this matter is resolved there is a hold on the will. I need to tell you more but not here"

Vera's face took on a serious note. "I hope they clear that matter up. Does this mean you're stuck here in the lap of luxury for awhile longer? Who do they think stole her identity?" Now Vera's lowered her voice.

"That's what I want to talk to you about. Somewhere else," Melissa whispered.

"We can have breakfast at a restaurant in Winter Harbor. It's not far from here. I had a slight accident and my car is in the garage."

"No problem. We can go in my car. I hope you didn't get hurt." Vera voice sounded concerned.

Melissa sipped coffee and relaxed in the rattan chair while Vera circled the room admiring the plants.

"Hello," Beverly said as she entered the sunroom. "Is this your friend Vera?"

"Yes, this is Vera."

Barry came by the sunroom, peeked inside and waved a greeting. He did not want to get involved in female chit chat so he continued walking down the hall.

"That's her husband Barry," Melissa stated.

"Did Melissa tell you she was in a car accident?" "We were worried about her for awhile

Beverly spoke in a concerned tone.

"Yes, I was lucky that a tree side swiped the vehicle, on the passenger's side, and stopped the car's momentum as it slid off the wet, dark, winding road," Melissa explained. "I feel fine now."

"May I join you ladies and have some coffee?" Beverly queried.

"Of course," Melissa said.

Sedwig entered the room, put a decorative tablecloth over the table then placed a fresh carafe of coffee on the silky cloth, exited the room with an empty coffee container. The display of freshly baked cookies had dainty, petite, dessert plates positioned next to them. Vera seemed to hesitate so Melissa picked up a napkin, and then selected a couple of cookies, which she put on the dessert plate.

Vera's eyes opened wide at the selection of goodies. She went to reach for a black/white coconut supreme square bar; however, Beverly's glare caused her to stop and follow Melissa's etiquette as she picked up a dessert plate and napkin. "This is great. Wow! Delicious."

Melissa thought her friend was not meant for this lifestyle.

Beverly seemed very talkative. The conversation veered toward the large selection of floral conglomeration, which adorned the sunroom.

"I used to run a floral shop," Beverly explained. "That's how I met Barry. He sent flowers to his ex-wife until he discovered there were other men sending flowers. They sent flowers from my shop also. If I told him sooner it might not have been such a shock when he caught her red handed. I felt sorry for him and after his divorce we got together and hit it off. I am so lucky to have him. I've talked too much. How about you? "She turned to Vera.

"To be honest with you," Vera replied. "I'm enjoying the snacks so much I really don't have much to say. I'd like to get the recipe. I am an amateur cook."

Melissa was relieved that Vera said little about herself.

"A whole family works in the mansion. The main cook is Jesse. Her mother and sisters do cleaning and other chores," Melissa informed Vera.

"Yes, as a matter of fact I need to check on the help. Thanksgiving dinner should be an elaborate event. Please excuse me." Beverly left the room.

Dinner was served at 6. Melissa and Vera went upstairs to their prospective rooms, freshened up and rested before the event. The snacks had worn off and both were hungry as they descended to the main floor, entering the dining room, where a delicious three course meal awaited them. The first course was served with an exquisite vinaigrette salad followed by crème of asparagus soup and roast duck with stuffing. Jesse brought out a freshly baked apple pie for dessert along with vanilla ice cream. Melissa tried not to look at her as she served the meal. Jesse's warning looks seemed to send out a message, which frightened her. Vera noticed Melissa's uneasiness when Jesse came out of the kitchen.

"We eat healthy here and exercise," Barry stated as he arose from the table after the meal. "Come along Beverly we need to go to the exercise room and work off the weight."

The comment embarrassed Vera who was overweight. "I have a thyroid condition so it's hard for me to lose weight,"

The couple left without any comment.

Vera commented to Melissa, "This is great! Thanks for inviting me."

Larry had been silent all through dinner; however, after he finished the meal, he became talkative as the three walked toward front room to get a glass of sherry. An after dinner drink had become a ritual. Melissa wondered whether Jesse's presence was the reason he was quiet at dinner. It seemed there was something going on between them. "I meant to tell you the repair shop called and you can pick up your car anytime. No charge. Celia left a stipend for you so that should cover the bill."

"Tomorrow is Thanksgiving Day. I can give you a ride the following day to pick it up," Vera offered.

Larry ushered the girls into the front room then poured three glasses of sherry and distributed them. The fireplace glowed with warmth and a feeling of relaxation seemed to enfold the room.

"I'm tired," Vera said as she placed the empty glass on the table. "It was a long drive."

"I'll take care of the empty glasses," Larry said as he collected them and went into the kitchen.

The girls walked upstairs together. Said good-night and went to their separate rooms.

Sylvie, the grey cat, curled up in a ball on the red velvet comforter. Melissa changed, slowly unrolled the cover and slipped into the newly laundered Egyptian cotton sheets. No sooner had her head hit the pillow a feeling of exhaustion seemed to encase her aching body and she fell asleep.

The next morning Melissa woke with someone tapping at the bedroom door.

"It's just me," Vera announced.

Melissa opened the door. Vera was dressed in a very fashionable pant suit set. Her hair was swept back in a pony tail and her eyes seemed to sparkle with excitement. "Happy Thanksgiving!" Vera announced. "The house aroma is filled with holiday cheer."

"I must've overslept," Melissa said as she yawned. "It probably won't matter if we're a bit late downstairs because Sedwig is busy preparing Thanksgiving Brunch along with Jesse's family. There will be no dinner just leftovers if we are hungry later. Wait here while I get dressed." Melissa selected a new outfit, from the closet, for Thanksgiving. Vera reclined on the bed and was amused by Sylvie showing off her cat antics.

Thanksgiving Day went smoothly. There were munchies, before the buffet was served and an ample display of various dishes at the luncheon. Assorted fruits, cheeses and a variety of desserts dotted the side tables. Larry made himself scare probably because Jesse was around. He ate in the kitchen instead of the dining room. Beverly and Barry selected health food items then excused themselves, from the dinner table, early as they headed toward the in-house gym. Melissa and Vera enjoyed the traditional turkey holiday meal.

"I can't eat another bite," Vera stated. "Let's go for a walk. I have been admiring the estate and would love to stroll around. It would be good exercise after the meal. Do you want me to clear the table?"

"No," Melissa replied. Sedwig would be upset. We need to wear warm coats and hats. The temperature dipped last night.

The girls bundled up in warm clothing and went outside.

"What's troubling me is how Aunt Celia could afford all this?" Melissa confided in her friend.

"I agree," Vera added. It's amazing how, on a bookkeeper's salary, your aunt could keep up this estate and have servants. Maybe her late husband left her a lot of money. The hired help seems to be part of her family."

"I'm not sure how Aunt Celia hired Barry and Beverly perhaps she advertised for caretakers to oversee the estate. Larry pretends to be divorced when I know he has a wife," Melissa revealed.

"Really! The whole situation seems like a mystery to me," Vera agreed.

"I'll tell you more when we go to breakfast tomorrow. I can't say too much now," Melissa concluded.

The subject was dropped as the two girls briefly circled the estate, and then headed toward the mansion due to the bitter cold. The fireplace blazed and emanated warmth, which both appreciated. After they felt comfortable Melissa ushered Vera into the library to select a book. They rushed back to the warmth of the front room where they reclined, one in a chair and the other on a sofa concentrating on their prospective novel choice. It was not until Larry came in clanging glasses and balancing a bucket of champagne that their concentration was broken.

Larry poured champagne into three glasses. He seemed a bit tipsy. "Let's make a toast to Thanksgiving and to Celia who made this feast possible. She was the most generous person. May her soul rest in peace?" Larry was starting to slur his words. He poured another round then sat by the fireplace in a recliner. Suddenly his glass fell to the floor. The two girls looked at each other.

"I think he passed out," Vera stated.

Melissa went over a picked up the glass. His breath reeked of alcohol.

"I guess you're right he is drunk. I think we should turn in early. You have to go back to college tomorrow," Melissa said.

"Yes, after we go to breakfast and I give you a ride to pick up your car I'm off to school,"

Vera informed.

They both rested comfortably and were up early the next day.

It was about an hour ride to Winter Harbor. A diner type restaurant sat in the middle of the town. It was plain but a big sign advertised "Home Style Cooking". Vera pulled into the parking lot. This time, of the year there were few tourists so they had plenty of vacant tables. A tall, older, grey haired woman greeted them. She seemed to be a cashier/hostess. Melissa pointed an area where there were no customers.

"That's closed; however, this table," she pointed to another area, "is available."

Melissa nodded in agreement noting the couple, at the next table got up to leave.

"We'd like coffee," Melissa requested of the young waitress, whom approached them.

She had short blonde fuzzy hair and a pencil tucked behind her ear. Her long face wore a frown but she forced a smile as she poured coffee. The white pale insipid complexion was a hint perhaps there was a health problem.

"We'll order later," Melissa stated. The waitress moved away from the table and stood near the coffee station anticipating an order.

"I think we are quite alone in here," Vera stated. "Now what's this mystery all about?"

"It's a strange situation at the mansion. No one is allowed on the third floor but Larry goes up there every night. When I awoke early morning, last week, I glanced out the window and saw him digging something up near the gazebo. He pulled a box out and started pulling papers out of it and stuffed them into his pocket then buried the container again. If that isn't suspicious the whole situation I uncovered in Augusta about Larry's wife is scary. I think she is the one that stole Aunt Celia's identity and perhaps embezzled money from the company," Melissa informed. Then she went on to tell her about Sally, the waitress in Augusta, and how she assisted in the inquiry to uncover the whereabouts of Larry's wife. Her name is Bertha Sanderson and she lives in Tampa, Fla. I have the address right here." Melissa pulled a notepad out and handed it to Vera.

Vera took the pad and tore the page out and handed it back to Melissa. "I have an idea," she said. "Christmas break I'll be visiting my parents in St. Petersburg. That is across the bridge from Tampa. I can go over there and check this lady out. I'll let you know what I find out. I'm ready for a home style breakfast. How about you?"

Melissa signaled the waitress to take their order. It was not a disappointment. As advertised a real home cooked breakfast. They ate in silence, paid the check and walked to Vera's car.

It was only a block away to the auto repair shop. Vera pulled up to the gas station.

"I don't think it's safe for me to send communications from the mansion. My cell phone doesn't work, at the mansion, so I will get a post office box here at Winter Haven," Melissa stated.

"Just send me an e-mail with a box number. Just the number and I'll know," Vera said.

The girls embraced in a friendly hug. "I hope you are safe at the mansion," Vera stated in a parting message. She waved as her car pulled out of the filling station lot.

Melissa went into Tom's Repair shop to pick up her vehicle.

"You're a lucky lady. Car still runs good," Tom remarked as he handed her the key. He was embedded with grease, from head to shoe, and busy so he quickly retreated to back of the repair shop.

Melissa remembered to go to the post office before leaving town.

CHAPTER 6

THE REVELATION

CHRISTMAS TIME, AT the mansion, was a spectacular event. A tall pine tree was placed in one corner, of the front room, emanating an aroma of fresh tar and pine throughout the house.

"Are there any volunteers to decorate this lovely tree?" Larry stood on a tall ladder, which enabled him to secure a multi-colored star on the tree top and arrange a string of lights strategically around the perimeter of the tree.

"I guess I will," Melissa offered.

Beverly entered the room with an armful of storage containers filled with Christmas decorations. She handed Melissa some ornaments to unwrap, affix hangers and attach to the Christmas tree. As Melissa hung the fancy hand painted balls she noted each one was inscribed by an artist. The glass blown balls, which depicted different paintings by Norman Rockwell, had been daintily autographed.

"Norman Rockwell signed these," Melissa stated in an excited tone. "Each depicts a scene from his famous art collection."

Sedwig entered the room and announced. "We will be having sandwiches for lunch."

The group was engaged in the tree decoration; therefore, ignored his presence. He left in a puff of anger. "I'm invisible around here," he muttered.

Larry pulled an angel decoration out of a box. "This looks a lot like you, Melissa," he grinned as he complimented her, then turned away and hung it on the tree.

Barry walked into the room. "This tree is one of the most beautiful I've seen lately," he remarked.

"I think the people who are decorating deserve some credit too," Beverly replied.

"Sedwig is getting a bit antsy. He is expecting the group for lunch. So it's best to go by his dining rules." Barry encouraged everyone to take a break.

The three stopped decorating the tree and followed Barry into the dining room. The sandwiches were made and other items were in a buffet style, which was the popular luncheon service these days.

"Jesse will not be here to prepare dinner because of the snow storm," Sedwig announced.

Melissa ate a small portion of food and returned to finish the tree project. It took a couple of hours to complete the job, even with the help of Beverly and Larry. After it was completed; she strolled into the sunroom to view outside. Snow was coming down and the whole ground was blanketed in white. She wondered how she would manage to get to the post office in Winter Harbor to pick up the mail.

Melissa started to feel tired. A nap would do her good. As she walked past the front room and peeked inside, a spectacular glow of the Christmas tree lights dazzled her. Larry had plugged the lights into the electric socket, which caused the tree decorations to glow in various colors and transform the room into a wonderland. The star twirled, on the tree top, and sent out beams of red and green light throughout the room, which reflected on the flames, in the fireplace and made them appear to dance in multi-color fashion. A sense of satisfaction seemed to overwhelm Melissa as she viewed the spectacular site; however, she didn't enter the room but continued upstairs to rest.

"Soup and salad will be served shortly," Beverly tapped on Melissa's bedroom door.

"I must've overslept," Melissa sleepily answered. "I'll be right down."

Sedwig seemed to be oblivious to Melissa's lateness for dinner, probably because it would be served buffet style. The heating plate, which kept the green pea/ham soup hot sat adjacent to the serving ladle. Everything Sedwig did was precisely arranged. The egg salad finger sandwiches were placed in a neat row, on a serving platter, which had a protective cover. A variety of bottle beverages floated in an iced tub. Plates, cups and utensils were conveniently placed next to the napkins. Barry and Beverly had eaten but Larry was still seated at the table. He had a ravenous appetite and could consume large quantities of food; therefore, he ignored Melissa when she sat across from him. When his food was completely devoured he glanced at her and watched until she was finished eating.

"Would you like to join me for a glass of sherry?" he asked.

Melissa followed Larry into the front room where the lit Christmas tree glowed and sent colorful rays throughout the interior. Melissa admired the view as she sat by the blazing fireplace and waited for Larry to pour a glass of sherry before confronting him.

"What if I told you someone informed me you are married not divorced?" Melissa asked.

"I'm not surprised. It's a long story," he replied.

"I'd like to hear about it," Melissa said.

"Well, it goes back to Augusta when I was married to Bertha. I am still married; however, there is a divorce pending. I hope it will be resolved soon. Anyway, I needed a job and I saw this ad in the Augusta newspaper so I applied and that's when I met your aunt. Celia informed me that the job was here in Station Harbor doing maintenance work on the mansion. Bertha was not happy about the separation but the money was good so she agreed. I commuted each weekend to Augusta to keep the marriage intact. One summer Bertha wanted to spend time here, at the mansion, so I asked Celia and she agreed. After Bertha came strange things started to happen. Some expensive jewelry Celia owned was missing also credit cards. I really think my wife has a mental problem or maybe she was jealous of Celia. Anyway, I sent her back to Augusta and filed for divorce. I think Celia reported the thefts to the police. I haven't seen Bertha for a year but she needs to appear in court to sign the divorce agreement. I really need this job so you can understand why I didn't tell you sooner. I hope you keep this quiet. The police are still looking for Bertha because of the stolen credit cards and jewelry. She is probably hiding out. The company, your aunt worked for, considered Bertha may be part of the embezzlement case."

"Oh," Melissa said. She was completely stunned by the revelation. "I won't say anything."

There was a slight noise near the door. Was someone listening?

Melissa dropped her guard and felt sympathetic toward Larry. She didn't know what to say.

They sat silently by the fireplace and soaked in the warmth, which emanated from the hearth while sipping sherry.

"I think this story deserves a second glass of sherry this evening," Larry said as he poured a refill into each glass.

As a good-night gesture Larry took Melissa's hand in his and said. "I think you are beautiful."

Melissa smiled. He is gorgeous she thought and soon single.

Melissa went up to her bedroom where Sylvie, the cat, was curled up on the comforter. She carefully picked the cat up and rolled down the bed. "You can sleep on the sheet," Melissa addressed the cat. "I'm getting attached to you. You like me better than Simeon does." She laid down, next to the cat, half dressed and fell asleep.

It was early hours of the morning when footsteps above woke Melissa. It was more than one person walking around.

Maybe Larry had a guest? Or maybe it was a dream? She was half awake and couldn't shake the drowsy feeling so she fell back into a deep sleep.

Next morning Melissa awoke to bright sunlight streaming in the windows. Sylvie, the cat, had strolled over to a comfortable chair and curled up in a ball. One look outside denoted that the snowstorm had abated and two feet was left by its aftermath. Larry was talking to a snow plow driver. It was the same guy who fixed her car. She remembered waking and hearing at least two people walking around upstairs. It could've been Larry and the mechanic? She decided not to strain her eyes glancing outside. The strong rays, of the sun, reflected off snow banks and momentarily blinded her. She dressed and started downstairs to get coffee and whatever delicacy Sedwig wished to offer for breakfast.

"Good morning," Beverly said as she eyed Melissa. "We have some delicious hot cross buns with our coffee this morning."

Melissa glanced into the kitchen and noted Jesse busily preparing Christmas dinner. She tiptoed into the kitchen and tried to avoid Jesse but before exiting with the coffee and bun. Jesse gave her another warning. She never looked up from basting the turkey but in a low tone. "Beware of Larry. He does not tell the truth. He may harm you." Then she became silent.

Melissa was about to say something but Jesse's mother came into the kitchen holding a duster and quietly walked past Melissa. Jesse seemed to tense up so Melissa left the kitchen with her coffee and bun. Jesse gave her another warning about Larry.

"We gave Sedwig Christmas Eve off since he has to work Christmas Day. Jesse and her family will have Christmas Day off. Sedwig will serve buffet style. I hope that is alright with you?" Beverly queried.

"That's fine," Melissa answered.

Jesse and her family were preparing Christmas dinner before the holiday. Sedwig would have to warm the meal up on Christmas Day. It seemed like a good plan. The aroma of turkey and dressing permeated throughout the first floor of the mansion along with the melding of fresh baked goods.

"There are some wonderful gifts under the tree. Barry likes to dress up like Santa. So after Christmas meal he will hand them out," Beverly explained. She motioned to Melissa to follow her into the front room where they could have coffee together and relax near the fireplace. Beverly turned on the tree lights to liven up the atmosphere and they both sat there inhaling the aroma from the fresh pine and enjoying the warmth from the flaming hearth. "I had to get away from the kitchen aroma. It made me so hungry and I need to keep on my diet."

Barry appeared with an armful of logs to place in the fireplace on the dying embers, which needed to be re-ignited. "Hope you two are keeping warm," he commented. "I have to take charge, Sedwig isn't here today." Barry seemed intent on starting the fire, which had diminished, so the room would return to acceptable warmth. He went over and turned up the heat thermostat. "Chilly in here," he commented.

"Barry is cold blooded. We have a home in Florida and hope to buy more property there. This year we couldn't go down there, as usual, because of Celia's death," Beverly explained.

Melissa wondered if the delayed reading of the will was one reason they stayed. After it was over would they return to Station Harbor or remain in Florida? She wasn't sure what connection they had to Aunt Celia. Perhaps they were just caretakers of the estate?

Christmas Eve was exciting. The numerous presents, under the Christmas tree, seemed to lend itself to a mysterious aura. What could be inside the packages? Melissa walked over and read a few tags. Some had her name on them; however, she dared not pick any up least she get caught in the act.

"Caught ya," Larry joked.

Melissa jumped, as her heart skipped a beat, at the surprise intruder's voice then laughed when she saw it was Larry.

"You can't peek. Santa will hand the presents out," Larry scolded.

Melissa turned around to see Larry standing there. He had cleaned up, shaved, and aroma of men's cologne encircled his body. He wore a casual top with cargo pants. How attractive!

"I dressed up a bit for the holidays. I still have to repair some plumbing upstairs. See you later." he stated as he exited the room.

Melissa stood silently admiring the tree but felt someone else was in the room. When she turned Jesse stood behind her.

"I would stay away from Larry," Jesse warned.

"Tell me why," Melissa said in a low tone.

"He belongs to someone else," Jesse answered in a whisper, then left.

I guess she means he is still married to Bertha? Maybe it was good advice. He is not free yet. Then the nagging doubts about him returned. Melissa went into the library to get a book to read in the sunroom and free her mind of present circumstances. She wanted to e-mail Vera; however, she would be visiting her parents in Florida. She wanted to ask Vera about Mark. Would he become interested in another girl in college or would he wait to see her in the summer? She picked up the romance novel, about two lovers who eventually got married, and Melissa became engrossed in the contents. It would have a happy ending.

Dinner was formal but a quiet occasion. Jesse served lobster bisque for the first course. Melissa managed to give her a slight smile feeling that Jesse might be concerned about her welfare in regards to a relationship with Larry. The main course was lobster tail with a special rice and corn. When dessert came Melissa was barely able to eat another bite. As usually, Beverly and Barry headed for the gym room. Larry bowed out of the glass of sherry saying he already had too much to drink. Melissa was relieved and decided to adorn her new winter jacket and take a walk around the estate.

Christmas day arrived. It was a bright sunshiny day, which caused some of the snow to melt and create ice puddles. Sedwig was dressed in his best attire for the occasion.

"I guess after breakfast and special home brewed coffee you will be attending church service with us? Beverly and Barry and I will be leaving shortly?"

"Yes," Melissa replied as went into the kitchen where a carafe of coffee was placed on the counter next to a variety of breakfast sweets, which encircled a side table. Christmas Day was special so she wore, one of the pantsuits, Mrs. James, the salesclerk recommended. The blue tone in the suit matched her eyes and brought out the lovely blonde locks she had created with a curling iron.

Beverly and Barry sat sipping coffee in the front room. Melissa joined them and admired their attire; each one complimented the other, with matching navy blue suits and stylish hats. Beverly smiled when she saw Melissa. "My, you look like a Christmas Angel, dear."

Sedwig came into the room announcing that the Cadillac would be leaving within five minutes.

"Isn't Larry coming with us," Melissa queried.

"No, dear," Beverly said. "He has some matter to attend to and he won't be dining with us either."

Melissa felt bit chagrin at the news. Was he spending the day with Jesse and her family she wondered?

The Christmas service was spectacular. The town pastor, Reverend Stanley, gave a great sermon. He even mentioned Celia in a tone of praise. How generous she had been and was truly a gift to the community.

After the service was completed, Reverend Stanley stood by the door. He wished everyone a great Christmas day. When Melissa came by the elderly pastor looked her straight in the eye and stated that she was so lucky to have such a wonderful aunt. If only she had met her.

When Sedwig drove Beverly, Barry and Melissa back to the mansion all was silent until Barry spoke. "Now I dress up as Santa and give out the gifts!"

Melissa relaxed, in the front room, by the Christmas tree with a cup of coffee. Beverly sat adjacent in a recliner. Sedwig stood by the door in anticipation of Barry showing up in a Santa suit. He would stand by and assist. "Perhaps," he commented "I should dress up also. As an elf and be Santa's helper." That was the first comical remark, Melissa thought, Sedwig made since she came.

Melissa was handed three gift boxes. "Who gave them to me?" she questioned.

"Your aunt, off course, selected these items before she died," Beverly stated.

Melissa opened the largest Christmas present first. It was a full length lambskin coat. The next present was matching hat and gloves. The third present was a cashmere sweater. All expensive and very stylish gifts her aunt had chosen, especially for her.

Beverly opened the gift that Melissa had bought in Augusta. Beverly smiled and thanked her. She loved jewelry. Melissa gave Barry and Sedwig key chains. They had been her father's; he left them in the glove compartment of the car. It would've been awkward if she didn't have a gift for them.

Beverly and Barry got combined gifts, which were from Celia before she died. Several electronic gifts were set aside for Larry. Sedwig and the other help received bonuses. Gift envelopes dotted the Christmas tree, with various names, denoting how generous Celia had been to all.

Food was displayed on a long buffet table and when anyone was hungry a self serve type of meal was available. Melissa ate Christmas dinner alone while the other members snacked at different intervals.

Larry came in late. He gave no explanation to his previous whereabouts on Christmas Day.

"I had to spend some time with you," he addressed Melissa. "Let's watch a movie in the library and have some champagne. It's getting late but we can enjoy what's left of Christmas together.

Even though she felt a bit tired from the long day it seemed like a good ending.

"I like old movies. This was one made, a long time ago, about the Black Dalia," Larry commented as he placed the iced filled champagne bucket on a stand. The two glasses, he was holding, made a melodic sound when he placed them on the table. He carefully poured the champagne and handed a drink to Melissa.

"Isn't that a murder that was never solved?" Melissa questioned about the film.

"Some women deserve to die. When they don't live right," Larry stated harshly.

It sent shivers down Melissa spine. Larry had a bad attitude.

Beverly and Barry peeked inside as the film started rolling.

"We're on our way to the exercise room. Want to say good night and hope you've had a nice Christmas," Beverly remarked. Barry gave a wave as they both walked away.

Melissa didn't want to see the movie. It wasn't a Christmas type of film. After the second glass of champagne she excused herself and said good night to Larry.

"What's your rush?" Larry questioned.

"The champagne made me sleepy and I need to go upstairs," she explained.

He put his champagne glass up in a toast position, "Merry Christmas!" Then took a drink and focused on the film.

CHAPTER 7

THE CATS GET KIDNAPPED

IT WAS NEW Year's Day. Melissa had spent New Year's Eve alone wondering where Larry was. He was not at the mansion and at the mention of his name, the members of the household, seemed to act strangely. Was he with Jesse and they didn't want to tell her?

Beverly mentioned everyone was invited to dine at a seafood restaurant, which Celia highly recommended and made reservations on New Years Day, before her demise. Melissa looked forward to an alternate dining experience, which she assumed would be totally opposite of the formal style that was a daily occurrence at the mansion. A husband and wife were owners of "On the Wharf" restaurant, which served home cooked meals with an oceanfront sea breeze and view. Celia had lent them money to start their business as an investment; however, the whole venture turned into prosperous undertaking. The restaurant became a popular tourist eatery in season. The couple, who ran the business, was grateful for Celia's generosity to make their dream possible and wanted to serve a New Year's feast to Celia's household members.

The restaurant was located in Station Harbor wharf area. The unique view was breathtaking even during the winter season. The white cap waves surfed ashore in an angry manner causing them to crash hard on the rocks and send streaks of water in several directions, and then a powerful suction pulled the water out to sea again.

The restaurant had a row of picnic style benches, which lined the middle section, then on each side small booths. It was not posh; therefore, Melissa felt more at home in this type of setting. A pot belly radiated heat throughout the interior, which seemed to keep everyone warm.

Mrs. Abernathy greeted the four at the door. "Welcome, to our little restaurant," she said. "You have oceanfront seats today, although the surf is rather rough it's a beautiful view. I think a storm is coming; however, this time of year it's to be expected."

The seagulls entertained the group by swooping down and devouring tiny morsels of food from the turbulent ocean.

"We love to feed the seagulls bread scraps," Mrs. Abernathy explained.

Mrs. Abernathy an oversized woman was dressed in a checkered dress and apron, which matched the table clothes and curtains in the restaurant. She waddled down the row of benches until she stopped at a table with a window view of the ocean. As she smiled her brown eyes crinkled up and emphasized her fat facial cheeks. "We are not opened to the public but have prepared a special meal; however, you can order something off the menu if you wish. What we plan to prepare is baked lobster tails. This time of the year the lobster shells are hard but we manage to open them and put a shrimp based stuffing inside. Does everyone like seafood?"

The group agreed.

Mr. Abernathy, the cook, identified himself through the kitchen server window. His face was elongated and clean shaven. A sprig of grey hair peeked out of his cook's hat, which sat lopsided on his head. "I'm Bill! You met my wife Sarah. Nice that you all could join us for New Year's Day," he spoke with a southern drawl.

Larry and Melissa sat, on a picnic style bench, opposite Barry and Beverly.

"Too bad Sedwig couldn't come with us," Berry remarked.

"Don't you remember? Sedwig is allergic to seafood," Beverly retorted sharply.

Sarah served several appetizers before the main course. The stuffed lobster tails, baked potatoes and fresh corn were delicious; however, when it came to dessert only Larry accepted.

"I can't eat another thing," Beverly stated.

"We're going to be in the exercise room all day after this meal," Barry commented.

Sarah came out with two pies. Does anyone want a dessert?" she asked.

"I'll have a piece of that crème pie," Larry said as he pointed to a pie in the display case.

"I think Beverly and I will stroll back. Thank you so much for the meal." Barry said.

Bill opened the kitchen door and waved. "I'm glad you'all came," he said with a southern drawl. Then he returned to the kitchen. Melissa observed that he was tall, thin and very congenial to his guest.

Sarah came over to chat while Larry devoured the pie.

"I hear you are Celia's niece? She gave so much to this town. Look across the street." Sarah pointed to the general store. "Celia gave that couple money to start the business and now it is prosperous. So many people, in this town, are indebted to her."

"Better get back," Larry said as he patted his stomach and got up to leave. Melissa followed him.

Bill opened the kitchen server door and said, "You all come back."

Sarah walked them to the door. "I'm honored to meet a relative of Celia," she said.

As Melissa and Larry walked down the narrow sidewalk, which led to the mansion Larry remarked. "You can tell that Mrs. Abernathy likes to eat."

"You should talk," Melissa chuckled. "The amount of food you eat: is piggish."

"It never shows," he said.

"I really enjoyed that meal and the couple made it a homey atmosphere," Melissa commented.

As they entered the mansion Mr. Clark, the lawyer, was standing in the hallway sporting a big smile. "Folks I have good news. The reading of Celia's will is going to be on February 4th. That would be her birthday, if she were alive."

"That's next month!" Larry voice was excited.

"The authorities feel the woman whom stole Celia's identity is responsible for the embezzlement. That means Celia is cleared of any charges. We will have to notify Leo since he is mentioned in the will. That will give everyone a chance to gather for the reading."

Melissa watched Larry's expression but it was blank. Even though it was his wife whom stole Aunt Celia's identity he probably still has some loyalty to her. Was he in cahoots with Bertha?

The snow plows finally cleared the road of snow and ice; therefore, Melissa decided to take a trip to Winter Harbor and check the mail at the post office box. Vera promised to check a few leads concerning Larry's wife location from an address in Florida.

The scenic road was now a winter wonderland with snow laden tree limbs, some fallen, other branches bent from the weight of icy conditions. On the ocean side the grey capped waves dashed toward shore then pounded on the beach. The sky, also grey, projected a dull glow as the sun made a weak attempt to peek through the clouds.

Melissa stopped, at a diner, for coffee and to get rid of the winter chill. She remembered the waitress from a previous time when Vera visited. The waitress approached to pour hot coffee. She moved swiftly and asked for a food order but Melissa only wanted coffee; therefore, the waitress moved on to another table.

Melissa finished the coffee and went to the register to pay. The waitress had taken on five or six tables and was in and out of the kitchen with several orders on a tray.

"She really moves fast," Melissa commented to the red headed teenage cashier with freckles and pigtails.

"Next year they are going to let me be a waitress," the squeaky voiced girl stated.

Melissa went to the post office. In the post office box was a letter from Vera postmarked from Florida. It stated:

Dear Melissa,

I went to the address you gave me in Tampa. I had to convince the landlady I was a friend of the occupant. I wasn't sure what name to use so I asked for Celia (not Bertha) and you were right. She was using a charge card with your aunt's name until last month. The trail grows cold. Seems she took off in a hurry and no one knows her forwarding address. She even left her belongings behind. I guess the police were at her apartment looking for her. I asked the landlady if I could go through her things but she had already packed them. Looks like Bertha's is in hiding. Hope this information helps but her whereabouts are still unknown.

Hope your holidays were enjoyable. I spent mine with my parents. The weather is here is great. I got a tan.

I heard from Harry. Harry and Mark are going to be working at the resort this summer. Mark sends his love. I think the guys are graduating from college this coming semester.

I am really worried about you at the mansion and the warnings you are receiving from Jesse. I hope you are alright and hope to see you at spring break.

Take care,

Love,

Vera

Melissa went into a stationary store and bought pen, paper and envelopes. She wrote a brief note to Vera inviting her, to the mansion, for spring break then mailed it.

As Melissa walked, out of the post office, a harsh winter wind swept through the lot, picking up debris particles and sending them through the air. She protected her eyes as she walked toward the vehicle. She had to get back to the mansion while the roads were clear. The sky showed signs of another storm brewing.

February arrived blanketed with ice and snow; which, from the bitter cold, encrusted on the ground. Leo and Nellie came, bundled in winter attire, for the reading of Celia's will. It was rather hard for Leo, with the inclement weather, to walk with his disability; however, Nellie pushed him around in a wheel chair. She had driven on a very treacherous road and was not in a good mood; however, smiled as she wheeled Leo into the study for the reading of the will. The other members, of the household, took seats situated around the room, which faced Mr. Clark's desk.

Mr. Clark sat in an oversized leather chair and waited for everyone to be seated, and then stood up and cleared his throat. "Is everyone ready for me to proceed?" He glanced around the room satisfied all eyes were affixed on him. He started to read the will.

From Celia:

"I want you to know I love each and everyone of you," he read.

"I leave the mansion and its contents plus an undisclosed amount of money to Larry for upkeep and bills, also the yacht."

The group turned and looked at Larry. He didn't seem to be surprised. Melissa felt a bit miffed because of his wife; however, she remained composed. Maybe Bertha would re-appear to claim part of the inheritance.

"To Beverly and Barry: My dear friends I leave a million dollars."

The couple looked at each other and smiled.

"Sedwig, a faithful servant for many years I leave a million dollars and a permanent job at the mansion."

Sedwig seemed pleased.

"To my niece, Melissa, I leave a million dollars."

"Jesse and her family should have a million split between them."

"They are not present," Mr. Clark said. "Jesse is cooking a delightful meal and will be advised later on that matter. She can notify her family."

"A half million goes to Leo. The million split between him and the cats."

"A half million goes in a trust fund for the cats Sylvia and Simon."

Leo's face dropped. "I have to share my million with two cats. That's not right."

"That seems to conclude the will," Mr. Clark said as he placed the paper on the desk.

"I think Jesse prepared prime rib, baked potatoes and green beans," Larry stated.

"You're always hungry. Congratulation on your inheritance," Melissa said.

"Let's all go into the dining room and have our meal," Mr. Clark suggested.

The room cleared except for Leo and Nellie. Leo leaned forward, away from the wheelchair, to address Nellie. "I'm not sharing my money with no cats," he slurred the words.

The dinner was delicious. Jessie had found out about the inheritance and she seemed to glide in and out of the kitchen with spectacular ease. Her family needed money and now they could afford to open a restaurant. Everyone was pleased with the will except Leo and Nellie. Their expressions were sour as they ate in silence.

"We can finally go to Florida," Barry said. "I've been so cold this winter."

Beverly smiled at her husband. "There still a lot of winter left here. I could stand some warmth myself."

After dinner, Barry and Beverly invited Leo and Nellie into the front room. Leo looked disgruntled. Nellie looked sad. Neither seemed happy.

Larry motioned Melissa into the library and poured their usual after dinner drink.

"I'll be glad when Leo and Nellie go back to their farm. They just don't fit with the rest of the family," Larry spoke low tone as he closed the library door.

"Where is the farm?" Melissa asked.

"It's on the outskirts of a small town located a few miles from Augusta. I think there are about 25 acres and a farmhouse. They hire some farm hands during the day. I think they many be illegals."

"They will probably leave tomorrow. Not happy campers with the will. By the way, did the police ever find your wife?" Melissa changed the subject after a knock on the study door.

Larry opened the door. Sedwig stood there with a bucket of champagne and two glasses.

"Thank you, Sedwig," Larry said as he accepted the gift then closed the library door. He turned to Melissa. "I finally got the legal verification that my divorce decree is final. Lots to celebrate," he continued as he poured the champagne into the glasses. "No, the police never caught Bertha but she can't use the credit cards anymore because they have been cancelled."

She can't collect half of my inheritance because we are no longer married. I finally got the divorce degree. As far as I'm concerned she can fade into the sunset. He lifted the champagne glass for a toast.

"To Celia," he said. Melissa joined in on the toast.

"What do you plan to do with your share of the money?" Larry queried.

"I plan to go back to school and graduate," Melissa replied.

"Stay here with me," Larry coyly invited.

"I'm not the type to live in a mansion. It's fabulous but I like a more informal atmosphere. You inherited a lovely home. What do you intend to do with the fortune?" she asked.

"I'd like to travel. Maybe go to France or Spain. Sedwig would be here to take care of the estate. Maybe I'll remarry?" Larry reached for Melissa's hand. Now he was single and rich. She didn't reject his touch.

"The champagne made me a bit sleepy," Melissa stated. "So many things happened today that I need to assimilate the situation." She picked up her glass and headed toward the kitchen. Somehow she knew Larry was going to drink well into the night and not be good company.

Melissa entered the kitchen where Jesse stood. Jesse never looked around but said in a low tone, "Stay away from Larry." Maybe she didn't know about the divorcee decree or maybe she wanted him. Whatever problem Jesse had Melissa was too tired to confront her so Melissa left the kitchen in a hurry imagining Jesse's hard stare as she exited.

Melissa past the front room and noticed Barry and Beverly seemed to have fallen asleep on the sofa. Barry had his arm around Beverly and they were cuddled close together. Melissa assumed Leo and Nellie had retired for the night so she tiptoed upstairs, so no one would be disturbed and fell asleep next to Sylvie.

In the wee hours of the morning Melissa awoke and heard a voice calling, "Here kitty, kitty." She assumed it was part of a dream and fell back to sleep. The exhaustion, of the day, had finally caught up to her; however, when she awoke Sylvie was not around.

Mr. Clark dispersed checks, sums of their inheritance, to everyone next morning. Leo and Nellie left shortly after not bothering to say farewell to anyone. They seemed in a hurry to get home.

"I'm glad they are gone," Larry stated.

Melissa munched on a pastry and drank coffee. "Are you and Jesse good friends or more?"

"What kind of question is that," Larry laughed. "I think she has the hots for me."

"She keeps telling me to stay away from you? I can't understand it."

"Can you blame her? I'm pretty hot stuff."

Melissa could not get a serious answer to the question.

Sedwig entered the room.

"Has anyone seen the cats? "he queried. I put food in their bowls. They always eat early morning."

"Strange, I had a dream last night that someone was calling a cat. Maybe it wasn't a dream," Melissa conjectured . . .

"I hope nothing bad happened to them," Larry stated.

"You don't suppose that Leo might dispose of them?" Melissa speculated.

"Leo was upset about sharing the million dollar inheritance with the cats. You think they took them?" Larry quizzed.

"We must not get alarmed," Sedwig stated. I did see Nellie placing some additional things in back of their old truck along with the luggage. I was busy in the kitchen so I don't know for sure if they were the cages with cats inside. When I looked out the window they took off so fast."

"We'll have to go to their farm and check it out," Larry stated. "We need to rescue the cats. Do you have plans for today?"

"Oh! The cats have been such good company all these years," Sedwig sadly stated.

Melissa put on an old pair of jeans, a shirt and a goose feather jacket with a hood then waited for Larry to pull the car around. They needed to inspect Leo's farm to see if the cats were there. Melissa had become fond of Sylvie and Simeon, Celia's two prize cats, and hoped no harm would befall them.

Larry drove for several miles before spotting the dirt road, which turned onto a village type setting with a row of disheveled buildings. A turn off, connected to another narrow road, was the direction toward the farm. Rocks and debris shot out from beneath the car as they traveled.

"I could never find this place. It's so rural," Melissa addressed Larry.

"Celia sent me out here a few times. I had to deliver money to Leo. That's how I know the directions. She was always giving him money. Now he resents sharing the fortune with the cats. Figure that," Larry responded. "Look! There's a place to eat. Want to stop before we get to Leo's farm?

"Yes, I'm chilled. The car heater keeps me warm but a hot cup of coffee would be great," Melissa said.

A young girl, probably 14 or 15 years old, stood behind counter. She had the face of a weather worn, older women—perhaps the make up and dyed blonde hair was a factor in the mature facade. The sparkle in her blue eyes reminded one of youth, which was quickly fading away.

"Do I know you? It seems like I've seen you before. What can I get you," she cooed.

Larry ignored the questions. "What's on special?"

"We have Sheppard Pie, fresh made," she replied.

They ordered the special and had coffee with the meal.

After the meal, Larry made a special request. "Could we walk, over to the barn, and take a look inside?"

"That would be alright," a voice from the kitchen said. It was the girl's mother.

"That was a delicious home cooked meal," Melissa commented to the mother half hidden in the kitchen. She looked as weather worn as the daughter.

"Come back anytime," the mother replied.

Larry took Melissa by the hand and led her toward the barn. He flung, the barn door, open. It was deserted. A tall hay stack encircled the barn. Larry reached out and pulled Melissa down on the hay with him. He came down on top of her and kissed her hard on the lips trying to unbutton her blouse. Melissa felt his strong body next to hers causing a magnetism she hadn't felt since Mark.

The barn door opened. An older, hunched back, stern faced man dressed in overhauls stood gapping at the couple.

"What you doin in here?" he asked.

Larry and Melissa felt embarrassed. No words were said. They exited the barn under the watchful eye of the farmer, departing swiftly from the awkward situation.

When they arrived at Leo's farmhouse it was getting dark. They parked, a short distance from the building, and walked the rest of the way until they came to the wrap around porch. Cautiously making their way onto the porch, crouching low to peek through the lighted kitchen window where Leo and Nellie sat having a cup of tea.

"Be careful! Larry cautioned Melissa. "He has guns."

The kitchen window was slightly ajar.

"What are we going to do with the cats?" Nellie asked.

"Gonna get rid of em," Leo replied. "Then I'm gonna put in for their share of the inheritance."

"When are we gonna do it," Nellie queried.

"In the mornin," Leo responded. "I bushed and gonna bed."

Nellie finished her cup of tea, then put both cups in the sink and wheeled Leo toward his bedroom. She put out the kitchen light; however, a dim glimmer of light, from a back room, streamed into the kitchen and brightened the interior. Two cat cages sat in a corner of the room.

"Meow, meow, meow." The cats were crying.

"I guess you are right. They did kidnap the cats," Melissa said.

"We have to sneak inside to rescue them. Leo and Nellie have to be sound asleep before we attempt it," Larry lowered his voice.

Melissa nestled next to Larry for half an hour. She felt warm as he put and arm around her and pulled her body close to his. It was cold and they needed to huddle together for warmth. Suddenly, he released the grip on her and motioned to follow him. He went around the side to view Leo and Nellie's adjoining bedrooms. He glanced into Leo's bedroom. He was sound asleep. Nellie was a different story she tossed and turned restlessly in her sleep.

"I think we can try to get the cats now," he instructed Melissa.

Melissa followed Larry around the farmhouse to the kitchen door. Larry pushed the squeaky door open. He stepped inside with Melissa close behind. Each footstep caused a noise as the floor board resounded with a creak. Larry went directly to the cat's cages. He grabbed Sylvie's cage and handed it Melissa, then he took hold of Simeon's container. The started toward the door for a quick exit with the cats, trying not to wake the two. They would not want to be caught as intruders.

Nellie half awake heard the floor boards creak. She was a light sleeper. "Who's out there?" She was coming to check.

Larry and Melissa ran out of the farmhouse, clutching the cat cages, racing toward the car.

"Uncle Leo wake up! Someone has broken into the house."

They were close to the vehicle when shots rang out. They threw the cat's cages inside and jumped into the car. Larry turned the key in the ignition then placed his foot heavily on the accelerator. As the vehicle sped away, from the farmhouse, rocks and flying debris shot out beneath the tires on the secondary road traveling toward the main highway.

It seemed like a never ending trip on the way home. There was nowhere to stop: at this hour most places were closed.

Darkness engulfed the whole area. The cats were restless due to ill treatment and lack of food. Larry hadn't spoken for most of the trip as the whole ordeal, still remained fresh in his mind. Both silently questioned whether it was worth the effort because they could've been shot. Melissa gave a sigh of relief when Larry turned into the mansion driveway.

Sedwig was still up as he rushed out to assist them with the cats. "I'll guard these cats with my life. Leo won't get near them again." Sedwig made up special dinner for the cats.

Melissa and Larry were exhausted, neither felt like talking. It had been a close encounter with death and against the law to break into a house; however, the cats were safe. That was all that mattered.

Sylvie was let lose and came upstairs with Melissa. The cat seemed to know that she was home again and curled up on Melissa's bed.

"I'm so glad that you were not harmed," Melissa softly petted the cat then drifted off to sleep.

CHAPTER 8

SPRING BREAK

VERA RETURNED TO the mansion, for a brief visit, during spring break. Melissa decided that Larry was fair game, after all, he was single; therefore, why not share the news with Vera.

In reality, the romance, hadn't reached full bloom and was mainly imaginary. Larry hadn't kissed her since the episode in the barn when they rescued the kidnapped cats. Melissa was still a virgin and didn't to be violated until marriage. Vera listened intently as Melissa related the events, which included the incident at Leo's residence.

"Larry is so sweet," Melissa stated. "Every time he walks by the sunroom he throws a kiss to me. Other times he leaves bouquets of freshly cut flowers."

Vera and Melissa were sipping coffee, in the sunroom, when Larry came in carrying a brilliant yellow bouquet of daffodils.

"For you," he said as he handed them to Melissa. "It's the first sign of spring." He turned to Vera and waved. "Good to see you again." Then he continued down the hall for some maintenance repairs.

"I told you last visit there was an attraction between you two," Vera said. "It shows! Your face lit up when he came into the room."

"I'm not too sure about Larry. We almost made love in the haystack. I am glad that farmer interrupted us because I don't want to go all the way with him. I plan to return to school and graduate before I either get tied down by children or a marriage. The funny thing, about the whole incident, is the farmer asked us what we were doing. As if he didn't know," Melissa chuckled.

"I hope you don't forget about Mark. He wrote a brief note and wanted me to deliver it," Vera stated as she took a card size envelope out of her purse and handed it to Melissa.

Melissa paused as she opened the note. In a low voice she started to read out loud.

"Dear Melissa",

"I haven't been able to get you out of my mind. I think I'm in love with you. I will graduate this year and have been offered a job at a location not far from your college. I acted impulsively and want to apologize. I would like to get to know you better and perhaps develop a serious arrangement in the future. You don't have to answer this note. Just think about us. I will see you at the resort this summer."

"Love, Mark

"Well, that sounds exciting. Harry will be coming to Maine, also," Vera commented.

"I think you are falling in love with Harry," Melissa joked.

"You might be right. He e-mails me daily," Vera replied. Vera then relayed a warning to Melissa. "Larry is now rich and single and perhaps has a relationship with Jesse? Have you thought about that?"

"I don't know Larry wouldn't give me a straight answer about their relationship. I think Jesse and family are going to open up a restaurant with the inheritance money. There are a lot of unanswered questions about Larry. Why would Aunt Celia turn over the estate to him?"

Beverly glanced into the sunroom and viewed Vera.

"It's a pleasure to see you again."

Beverly turned to Melissa.

"Barry and I are going to Augusta to make travel arrangements for Florida. That money we inherited will come in handy. I think we will fly down to sunny Florida, store the car in the airport garage for a few months and return when the weather is better."

"When do you plan to leave?" Melissa inquired.

"In about a week," Beverly replied. "The daily routine, at the mansion, will change now that Larry is in charge. The protocol will be will be less formal. Jessie and her family have purchased an old restaurant structure and are restoring the building. It's there first business venture. Sedwig will do a lot of serve yourself meals. Looks like it will be you and Larry." Beverly concluded the conversation and waved, at the girls, then followed Barry, whom had been patiently waiting in the background, to the gym room.

"Are you sure you want to stay in this big house with Larry and Sedwig? It will be spooky or maybe you want to get better acquainted with Larry?" Vera quizzed.

"The resort restaurant opens in about six weeks. We can rent an apartment, at the same complex as last year, and start working as soon as it opens. Don't worry about money. I can use some of my inheritance until we start making tips. I want to use the rest, of the money, to graduate," Melissa stated.

Sedwig appeared in the doorway.

"Master Larry and I are going to a town meeting today. The coffee carafe is full. There is plenty of food in the refrigerator." Sedwig left quietly.

Melissa glanced out the window to see a limo pull away. "I guess Sedwig wears many hats in this household. Now he is a limo driver."

Vera came to the window and viewed the limo until it was out of sight. "I've never seen a limo before. I hope this glitter isn't going to your head."

"Not really. I enjoyed a real home cooked meal the other day at a run down eatery. They served Sheppard's Pie and it was delicious. The old self emerged. The food here has been elegant; however, I've always felt ridged at the table. Afraid I might drop a folk or stain the tablecloth. It puts you under a strange pressure no matter how good the food might taste," Melissa stated. "While everyone is away I'd like to explore the area near the gazebo where Larry digs up something then places a shrub over the top. It will be easy to find since it is fresh dug dirt."

Vera followed Melissa outside to the tool shed. Shovels leaned against the wall, of the wooded structure, in a haphazard manner. Melissa handed Vera a shovel and grasped the handle of a second one, which caused a whole row of tools to scatter. "I hope Larry doesn't notice. Follow me," Melissa said as she strolled over to the gazebo. "We have to carefully remove this shrub to uncover the mystery that lies beneath."

Before the dig, both girls glanced around to ensure they were not being watched. All seemed safe as they started the dig. Not long into the process a hard object was discovered. Their shovels dug easily into the porous ground, which had been turned over several times.

"Here's the box!" Melissa said excitedly. She brushed dirt off the top, and then opened the container. The money she witnessed was packed solid except for a wad of cash, which fell out and landed on the ground. Vera was awe struck as she glanced into the box and saw several compartments, which were filled with money of different denominations, one hundred, five hundred and some thousand dollar bills secured with a clip. Melissa cautiously returned the wad of cash to the container, fastened the clasp then quickly returned it to the open hole. Silently the girls started covering up the box realizing the money discovery may be dangerous to them.

"Now we know where Larry keeps his bank account," Vera commented. "We covered the hole just in time. Listen! I hear a car coming up the drive. We could get into trouble. After all, this is Larry's estate."

The two girls worked like clock work by placing the money box back in the hole and covering it with a shrub then spreading the soil over the burial spot. They rushed over to the tool shed, spot cleaned the shovels; however, did not have time to tidy up the room.

"Hurry! "Melissa yelled. "It's not Larry but Leo and Nellie! They're going to make another attempt at kidnapping the cats. It's all because of Aunt Celia's will. She left the cats half million, in trust, and Leo feels the money belongs to him so he wants to kill them and take their share of the money.

Both girls rushed into the back door of the mansion while Leo and Nellie pulled up in front.

"Grab one of the cats. I'll get the other." Both cats were napping in the sunroom. Melissa got their cages and placed them safely inside. Simon objected to the transfer with a few meows but Sylvie calmly curled up inside the carrier.

"Let's take them upstairs," Melissa instructed. "We'll pretend no one is home."

The girls barricaded themselves in Melissa's upstairs bedroom placing the cat's carriers under the bed. They watched, out the window, carefully screening their view to outside.

Leo's old vehicle came to a screeching halt at the front door or the mansion. Nellie stepped out of the driver's side. "I don't think anyone is home," Leo called out to her. "We can break into the house and get those cats."

Nellie rang the bell. No answer. She picked up a rock and threw it through a front window. The sound of crashing glass resounded throughout the mansion.

"I think they are breaking in," Vera whispered to Melissa. "Go lock the bedroom door."

They heard them rummaging around downstairs.

"I don't see the cats down here. Go upstairs and check," Leo's voice was loud.

The girls froze as the footstep came closer. Someone was turning the door knob.

"Dammed it!" Nellie's harsh voice sounded mad. "The rooms are locked."

The girls held their breathe hoping the cats wouldn't let out a sound. Each cat seemed to be asleep in their cage. Finally, the footsteps seemed to be descending the stairs.

A police car pulled up in the front driveway in back of Leo's car. Two cops got out.

One recorded the license plate of Leo's car. There was a knock on the front door. Melissa opened the door to the bedroom, cautiously descending the stairs watching for the pair. The coast was clear, so she opened the door for the two policemen. Leo and Nellie had seen the police car and exited out the back door.

"Did you call about a break in?" One of the cops asked.

"No, but someone put a rock through the window." Vera said as she came down the stairs and saw Melissa standing in the entry hall with two policemen.

"They got into the house," Melissa added. "They are relatives but have not business here."

"It must've been a neighbor that called. We'll have to write a police report," the tall cop stated.

"Hey! Stop!" the second police sergeant shouted as the old vehicle took off in a puff of smoke. "Those two are escaping." Nellie and Leo had gone out the back door, sneaked around the front then jumped in their car and took off.

The stocky built police sergeant took the statement. "I have their license number. We'll get them later. Anything missing?" he asked.

"We haven't checked yet. I think they were after the cats." Melissa said.

"Cats!" The policeman looked at each other with a smirk. "My cat had a litter. They can have one or two of mine."

"You don't understand. These cats are worth a half million dollars. My aunt left the money in a trust fund for them. Leo and Nellie were unhappy about their settlement so they wanted to kill them and get the cat's share of the money." Melissa tried to explain so it wouldn't sound too ridiculous.

Another policeman, on a motorcycle, pulled up. "I just got this call. We are in pursuit of the vehicle." Officer Bill was dressed in a special unit's police garb. His side burns and mustache emphasized his short hair. "We're going to put a restraining order on them. They won't be bothering you or the cats again," he said in a firm tone.

The three policemen huddled together, outside the mansion, and had a discussion before departing.

"That was strange," Melissa addressed her friend. "I wonder who reported the break in."

"Whoever it was we can be thankful. I think Leo and Nellie have some issues. Leo might have pulled out a gun and forced us to give up the cats." Vera replied.

"He did shoot at Larry and me; however, we did break into his farmhouse to get the cats that night. Maybe that was a get even move on their part? I do feel sorry for Leo. He has lack of money and health problems. After the police scared them I doubt they'll come back," Melissa stated.

They dropped the subject. The cats were released from their cages.

"Let's raid the refrigerator," Melissa said. A carafe of hot coffee was on the sideboard.

They brought the food into the front room and sat in front of a TV. Melissa turned on a romantic movie. "I rarely come into this room. It's usually been reserved for Beverly and Barry."

"Things are changing. Let's watch TV. You've missed some good soap operas. A person could get spoiled around here. Sedwig made up the most delicious finger sandwiches," Vera remarked as she relaxed in the plush green chair and devoured the food.

A vehicle pulled up. It was Larry and Sedwig returning from the town meeting.

Larry seemed pleased as he spoke about the meeting. "Well, I guess the town council approved some new businesses in town. This place is growing like a weed. I'm going to invest in some additional financial ventures. We are going to make this town a tourist attraction. There are a lot bucks to be made in season."

"I'll work in one of your restaurants," Vera offered.

"I'll let you know when I own one," Larry replied.

"We've had some excitement today," Melissa stated. She explained how Leo and Nellie broke into the house. "The police showed up and put a restraining order on them."

"That's good," Larry reasoned. "They won't bother the cats again or they'll go to jail."

He went into the kitchen where Sedwig was setting up dinner. They spoke in low tones. Larry grabbed a cup of coffee as he sat, on a kitchen stool, and consulted with Sedwig on some serious issues. They seemed to have a lot to discuss.

Beverly and Barry came home.

"We'd better go into the study and let them have the front room," Melissa stated.

Dinner was served buffet style. The formal dining was still in vogue mainly because Beverly and Barry were around. The meal had been rapidly prepared and not as good as usual. The girls were not hungry after snacking all day.

After dinner, Melissa and Vera relaxed on a silken sofa. Larry came in and handed each a glass of sherry. He invited them to toast on his good fortune.

"The dinner was not great but the sherry will make up for its inadequacy," he said as he lifted his glass.

"I guess the meals will be informal when Beverly and Barry leave. Jesse is a great cook," Melissa remarked.

"I saw her today," Larry made a slip of the tongue. He didn't elaborate on the circumstances. Maybe it was his girlfriend?

"Maybe you'll invest in her family restaurant?" Vera made a sarcastic remark.

"Maybe," Larry said as he poured the girls a second round of sherry. He drank in silence then corked the bottle.

"Please excuse me," he said. "Tonight I am tired. Good night ladies." He bowed then left.

"I think that's our cue to retire," Vera interjected.

"You're right," Melissa replied as she followed Vera upstairs. Melissa said good-night to Vera and walked down the hall toward her bedroom. Sylvie was curled up on the bed comforter.

"Thank goodness no harm came to you," Melissa said softly to Sylvie as she stroked her fur. Sylvie purred as if she understood. Melissa tossed and turned before falling asleep uneasy about Larry's relationship with Jesse and the unexplained money.

The week Vera spent, at the mansion, passed by fast. It was time for Vera to go back to school.

Melissa walked her friend to the car and gave her a friendly hug.

"Its good bye until another six week," Melissa sad voice recanted.

Vera seemed concerned about Melissa welfare. "Are you sure you don't want to come back with me? You can stay at my parent's place. "I heard footsteps, on the third floor, last night."

"It was probably Larry," Melissa tried to comfort her friend.

"I don't think so," Vera said. He was outside digging up that box. I hope he didn't catch on to our snooping. Maybe he ran out of money?"

"I've never been up on the third floor. Once I did try the door and it's locked."

"I might start sounding like Jesse but I would be careful," Vera cautioned. "She might be warning you about someone or something. I noticed she quit her job here."

Melissa's face took on a sad appearance. This was her friend. She did need to heed her warnings.

"Don't forget if things get too out of control here go to my parent's house. They will be in Florida for awhile. The key is under the front door mat. They won't mind if you stay there."

Vera got into her car and pulled away.

Melissa stood there and watched her friend's car until it was out of sight.

CHAPTER 9

THE EPISODE

THE ARRIVAL OF spring ushered in a change of season as warmer days seemed to return; however, winter's memory remained in the form of a cool breeze, which seemed to linger. The time change allowed longer days and plenty of sunshine to ensure the rebirth of the tulip bulbs and other seedling, which hid beneath the earth for protection through the harsh winter.

Sylvie, the cat, followed Melissa around the estate. Sylvie curled up next to her as Melissa read a mystery magazine while reclining on the gazebo bench. The cool spring breeze blew through the enclosure and caused Melissa to shiver. She reminisced about Mark. Maybe there would be a future with him? The summer was around the corner and she would see him again. A feeling of elation uplifted her at the thought of seeing him again. The wind, picked up strength, and blew debris around. Melissa picked up the cat, placed the book under her arm and proceeded toward the mansion bracing against the onslaught of dirt and other particles, which flew through the air. "It's too windy out here," she said to Sylvie.

Beverly and Barry were glad to see her. They wanted to say farewell as Sedwig loaded luggage into their car.

"We might not see you again," Beverly said as she hugged Melissa.

"We wish you the best of luck," Berry added.

Melissa and Sedwig waved but felt sadness as the married couple departed. "They were an intricate part of the household," Sedwig commented. "Nothing at the mansion will be the same."

It was odd, Melissa reasoned, they said farewell. Perhaps they planned to stay in Florida?

Melissa looked around the mansion. It seemed vacant now.

Larry came up to her. "It's just you, me and Sedwig."

Sedwig stated, "Now that the household had so few members it will be self service. I will make sure the refrigerator is full and you serve yourselves. The dining room is officially closed. Jesse and her family have purchased a restaurant. You can go there and dine."

Melissa did not want to hear anymore warnings. It was a fat chance of her eating there.

"I have some maintenance repairs but we can take a picnic lunch out on the yacht," Larry offered. "The weather is supposed to get milder in a day or so."

"I don't have any plans," she replied.

Melissa secretly wanted to check the post office box at Winter Harbor. It was boring at the mansion. No one to chit chat with, no fine dining and books were getting boring. She read most of the choice selection in the library. A brisk walked through the garden would wake her up. The air was cool; however, warmth seemed to permeate the air and mediate the temperature. There were Romanesque statures dotting the garden. A row of delicately painted benches encircled the figures and a huge fountain stood in the center of the marble encrusted patio.

She could hear footsteps behind her.

"Hello, I'm Morris the gardener," a squeaky voiced man spoke.

She looked around to see a very petite fellow, perhaps a midget, with a mustache and slicked back hair style. His dark complexion emphasized the big brown eyes.

"No one has mentioned you," Melissa stepped back startled.

"I'm just a seasonal worker. Just here to see what plants to order and to maintain the garden through the summer season." The tiny figure inspected the foliage then disappeared through the shrubs.

Melissa thought to herself. I guess Larry intends to carry on Aunt Celia's tradition and keep the grounds well maintained. The upkeep must be expensive. Melissa had to think up ways to keep busy throughout the day; however, she planned to go to Winter Harbor the following day to sightsee and explore the area. When school starts who knows when she will have time to return?

The sleepy town of Winter Harbor seemed to have awakened since January. Hotel, motels, restaurant and stores had opened. Melissa stopped at the same restaurant although, the opening of tourist season, brought other coffee shops to life. A waitress approached with hot coffee pot and as she bent over to pour coffee Melissa read the name inscribed on the name tag. Pam did not move away swiftly this time she stood and encouraged Melissa to have breakfast. The thin, tall waitress didn't seem to have the same energy. She remembers her, on the last trip to Winter Harbor, to be energetic.

"I think I recognize you," Pam stated.

"Yes, I've been here before. I'll have French toast. How have you been?" Melissa asked.

"Not to well. I had to have some surgery to remove my gall bladder. I hope that doesn't gross you out," Pam said as she tore the order off the pad.

"No, I notice you had quite a heavy load waiting on 5 or 6 tables last time I was here," Melissa spoke.

"They are hiring more waitresses. Thank goodness," Pam called the order through the server's window.

After Pam served Melissa the French toast and refilled her coffee cup, she let to wait on a bus load of tourist who had arrived. Melissa was hungry. She hadn't eaten much the previous night and now was famished.

Pam returned with the check. "Where're from?"

"Station Harbor," Melissa replied.

"I remember that town. That's where that rich old lady died. The rumor had it that she embezzled money from some company in Augusta. Glad she was innocent. They never found out the guilty person." Pam moved to another table. Melissa got up and paid the cashier. She was relieved that information about her aunt was short and sweet; however, gossip travels quickly.

The stroll along the beach walk way in Winter Harbor was windy and cold. The sea surf pounded toward the shore as high tide took over a massive amount of sandy beach. Melissa stopped at souvenir shops along the way to get away from the wind swept tide, then suddenly decided to return to Station Harbor. She checked the post office box and found a letter from Vera.

As she entered the mansion a cold, dark, and deserted scene made her shutter. The fireplace embers sparked and only a flicker remained lit, leaving the front room damp and cold. Lamps, throughout the house, were unlit. Melissa felt it was time to leave. Perhaps this was a hint. Sedwig's absence unnerved her. Larry was no where to be found. It seemed spooky in this huge dwelling without the household members. She clutched the letter from Vera and decided to go into the sunroom to read the contents. The solar panels, in the room, emanated warmth and light throughout, the whole area.

She read:

> Dear Melissa,
>
> I've returned to school but still concerned about your safety. The offer, I made, about my parent's residence is still an option for you. They won't return until late June and you can stay there until the restaurant opens and we can share an apartment at the resort. It will be just like last summer.
>
> Harry calls me every week. He is going to graduate and teach, in a school, not far from our college. I think our relationship is getting serious or maybe that's my wishful thinking.

I am looking forward to seeing you soon.

Love,

Your friend,

Vera

Melissa put the letter down and reasoned: I guess that's what I'll do. Go to Vera's parent's house and stay until the summer resort opens for the season. She went upstairs, closed the bedroom door then lay down next to Sylvie and slept. Melissa awoke, early morning to shuffling feet on the third floor. Several people seemed to be moving around. What were they doing up there? She glanced at Sylvie, curled up, which seemed to put her at ease and she went back to sleep.

Larry seemed pre-occupied most of the week; however, when the week end rolled around and the weather improved the idea of a picnic and a cruise resurfaced. It was a gorgeous day. He packed a picnic lunch and took Melissa by the hand and led her to the dock, where they cautiously climbed down the rugged cliff ladder to the anchored yacht. The sky was clear blue with a few clouds floating by, which allowed sunlight to filter through at different intervals.

The yacht rocked back and forth in a rhythmic motion, which affected the waves and caused them to crash against the side, of the vessel, in an unsteady motion. Larry assisted Melissa as she boarded the vessel. He put a skipper's cap on his head then rushed to the engine room and set the automatic pilot on full throttle. It lunged forward, separating the water as its powerful force maneuvered forward. Larry slowed the engine, and then put it on idle as they entered an isolated inlet and came to a stop.

"Are you hungry?" he quizzed.

"Yes, I haven't had anything to eat since yesterday," Melissa replied.

The swanky interior, of the yacht, impressed Melissa. She observed more, of the interior, than in the previous cruised around the area. Aunt Celia loved red and it was reflected in the decor. Red satin seats, red draperies and richly designed integrity fashioned red rugs. The kitchen had the latest red toned appliances.

"I brought a couple of bottles of champagne," Larry said as he pulled them out of the picnic basket along with sandwiches, potato salad and macaroni salad. In a separate container were glasses, plates and utensils.

"You thought of everything," Melissa said.

"To be honest with you I didn't prepare this meal Sedwig did," Larry said as he poured the champagne. He handed her a glass of champagne. Then lifted the glass for a toast, "To us," he said. Melissa joined along not realizing the implication.

"What are we toasting to?" she asked. "The house is so gloomy, dark and cold. It's not like before. I really don't feel welcome.

"Things are different now. Sedwig spends part of his time in the servant's quarters. I'll show you sometime where he maintains a separate residence."

Melissa took a bite out of the sandwich. "He makes delicious sandwiches."

"Sedwig made a nice lunch for us," Larry agreed.

Larry poured another glass of champagne; which finished off the first bottle.

They continued to feast on the luncheon. Larry uncorked a second bottle of champagne.

"I feel strange. A little dizzy. I hope I'm not getting sea sick," Melissa said weakly.

"Come downstairs and rest," Larry instructed.

Melissa allowed him to assist her in the descent downstairs. Red velvet decor lined the interior of the plush bedroom. He laid her down, placing her head, on the soft velvet cushion then situating her body on a silk bed sheet that had been turned down.

"You'll feel better if your clothes are loosened," he said as he started undressing her.

She tried to resist; however, weakness overcame her as he unbuttoned her blouse and unzipped her jeans. The champagne had taken its affect and she passed out. The rest of the experience would never be remembered and probably just as well since she was violated against her will. Melissa allowed herself to be duped by Larry.

Time passed and she finally came around. "Did you lace my champagne?" she asked.

He didn't answer but the evil laugh answered the question. "Get dressed," he said gruffly. "We're going back to the mansion. If you tell anyone about this incident I'll deny it ever happen." His whole character seemed to change. Like Jackal and Hyde. The engine was placed on full throttle and he ignored Melissa as they raced back home. She felt shaken by the experience but who could she confide in? When they reached the shore he anchored the yacht, carried the picnic basket up the step rock stairway leaving Melissa to fend for her. She still felt a bit dizzy and drunk. She was probably doped up.

As they entered the mansion he remarked, "You're immature and stupid. Maybe you learned a lesson. You'd better go to bed and sleep off the liquor. It's a good thing Sedwig isn't around."

Melissa stumbled upstairs by herself. The drink and drug had an effect on her. She slept soundly until early morning but woke with a sick feeling and had to vomit. She vowed never to trust Larry again. Now she remembered Jesse's warning.

The next morning Melissa heard Sedwig humming in the kitchen. Her stomach was still a bit queasy; however, she would attempt to hold down a cup of coffee. Her courage returned and she would not discuss or show the distaste for Larry that she now felt. Like an actress she hid her true feelings then entered the kitchen to pour coffee.

"Where is the location of the restaurant Jesse and her family plan to open?" Melissa quizzed.

"It's near the wharf but not on the ocean front. It's called the New Day Restaurant. I don't know if the repairs have been completed but you can check," Sedwig replied.

"I think I'll have lunch there if it's open," Melissa stated. "I am leaving tomorrow. I need to get ready for school."

"You'll be missed by me and I assume Master Larry," Sedwig replied.

Melissa stayed silent as she sipped the coffee and headed toward the sunroom. The house was still dark, however, Sedwig lit a fire in the front room fireplace. The house felt warmer when he was around. She was glad Larry was absent. Tomorrow she would be rid of the uneasy feeling of his presence. How dare he do that to her and take something precious without permission. She picked up a book and started reading taking her mind off the uninvited experience.

Lunch time arrived. Melissa dressed in a pantsuit and neatly arranged her blonde hair in an up do, then took off for the New Day Restaurant hoping to find Jesse. What was she to say? She had not heeded the warnings?

The restaurant sign stated "Grand Opening Saturday"; however, Melissa walked inside the building and looked around. Was Jessie here? A few tables and chairs dotted the interior. The rugged structure once an old log cabin breakfast eatery was being converted into a lunch and dinner restaurant.

Jesse came out of the kitchen. "Please come in and sit down. We are not really opened for business but I made a nice lunch for the workmen. I think you would enjoy the beef stew," she said. Then she went into the kitchen and came out with a bowl of stew; which was steaming hot, then placed a spoon and napkin nearby.

There were men, on the roof, making repairs. The noise was a bit bothersome but Melissa wanted to spend a few minutes with Jesse even if the sounds were annoying. She carefully sipped the stew. Jesse sat opposite and smiled.

"This is delicious. I've enjoyed your meals tremendously at the mansion. I'm leaving tomorrow and wanted to thank you," Melissa stated.

"No doubt you are going to ask me about my warnings to you," Jesse inquired.

"No, that was answered yesterday, "Melissa said sadly.

"He drugged and violated, you too! I'm so sorry," Jesse looked forlorn. "I don't think either of us could do anything about it. This town would ostracize us if we told the truth."

"I just wanted you to know I appreciated your warnings even if I didn't heed them."

Melissa finished most of the stew and then got up to leave. Jesse sat silently twisting a plastic coffee stirrer. It was a nervous gesture reliving an experience she was unable to justify.

Jesse walked Melissa to the exit and cautioned about workmen's nails and boards scattered on the floor. The girls hugged. Melissa wished her the best of luck with the restaurant then walked back to the mansion.

Larry was waiting. "I hear you're leaving tomorrow," he said.

"Yes, I'm going upstairs to pack," Melissa answered coolly.

"Before you leave, I have a surprise for you," Larry stated.

"I think you've given me enough surprises. I'm not interested in anymore," Melissa moved past him and started up the stairs.

"I think you'll be interested in this one," Larry called out.

Melissa kept going. What did he mean?

CHAPTER 10

FULL DISCLOSURE

THE SOFT MORNING breeze trickled through Melissa's partially opened bedroom window, and caused the red satin curtains to blow around. The corner, of a curtain, hit a porcelain ornamental statue located on a side table and it crashed on the floor. Melissa awoke suddenly and viewed the object, which was scattered in several pieces. She quickly hopped out of bed and retrieved the various remnants, of the stature, and placed them in a plastic bag.

A memory of a bad dream or perhaps a nightmare or a bad dream drifted through her mind. No, it wasn't a bad dream. Had really happened? Yes, Larry had taken advantage of her on the yacht. It didn't mean anything to him since he also violated Jesse. She brushed away a tear. The suitcase, on a vanity bench, sat opened and ready to pack. After Melissa showered and selected an appropriate outfit for the drive to Vera's parent's residence she quickly filled the suitcase, closed the suitcase, carried it downstairs and placed it near the door.

An aroma of bacon and coffee awoke her senses as the odor wafted through the air. Somehow it was a signal Sedwig was preparing a special breakfast. She entered the kitchen and noticed the butler's plastic expression had softened. Sedwig had a human side too.

"I made a special breakfast for your departure. Sit down and eat," he said softly. "I'll never accept Larry's marriage," he muttered. "He might run the estate differently. I don't know."

"Is he going to get remarried?" Melissa quizzed.

"I'm afraid so. It might even happen today," Sedwig stated sadly. "It's someone on the third floor. He wants you to meet her before you leave."

Melissa stiffened at the request; however, her curiosity got the better of her. After breakfast Larry came into the kitchen.

"Come with me," he stated. "I'd like you to meet my future bride."

"Not without Sedwig," Melissa retorted sharply.

Sedwig made up a tray, which consisted of a coffee carafe with two cups and a muffin then followed the two upstairs.

Melissa wanted to shout at Larry and tell him off but Sedwig was in back and she didn't want him to know what had happened so she held her tongue and quietly followed Larry up three flights of stairs. Sedwig observed the friction between the two. Larry was rigid in his behavior, not at all himself. He leaned close to Melissa, "Not a word about what happened if you know what's good for your health." They reached the top, of the third floor, where Larry slipped a key into a lock and motioned Melissa to enter first. A strong aroma of lavender perfume emanated throughout the area.

The third floor was turned into a small apartment. It had a kitchenette, living room, bathroom and a room, off to the side: an office with a computer and telephone placed on an old oak desk. Larry led them inside the tiny office. A woman sat in a high back desk chair peering out the window as if surveying the estate. Only the back of the woman's head was visible as the auburn tinted hair appeared above the chair. Its lovely tone glowed in the sunlight. Slowly the swivel chair turned around and the woman faced the three. Melissa gazed at the stylish auburn haired women with hazel eyes and firm skin. Diamond earrings sparkled as they swayed at her every movement. The necklace, which matched her earrings, hung in a fashionable manner at the neckline of her red cashmere sweater.

She extended her hand to Melissa. The red meticulously manicured fingernails matched the color of the cashmere sweater. On her middle finger was a huge smoky topaz ring encircled with diamonds.

"I'm your Aunt Celia," she said.

At first Melissa was lost for words; however, her composure returned. "You look so young. My mother was 50 and you're her older sister," Melissa stated in amazement as she accepted the out stretched hand in greeting.

"I know dear. The calendar years don't matter. I've had a face transplant, skin graft and reconstructive surgery, done in Eastern Europe and now I'm a different person with a new identity. Larry and I are to be married today. I know how shocked you are. Larry will make plans now that I am fully healed from all the surgery.

"No way can I pull wedding plans together so fast," Larry objected.

Celia turned to Larry ignoring his objection, "Call Jesse and her family for the food service at this gala event. Call the pastor and see if he is available to perform the ceremony. Leave right away and set things up. We have guest to invite."

Larry looked stunned. It was a sudden decision on Celia's part.

"Will I be able to buy that new sports car?" he queried.

"When the wedding ceremony is over," Celia stated.

Larry coughed nervously as he left the room. He gave Melissa a menacing glance.

Sedwig looked upset. When Larry was gone he blurted out his displeasure, "For years you and I had an intimate relationship. Alfred never caught on to our love. Now you decided to marry Larry. I don't understand." Sedwig said. His hands shook as he placed the tray on a side table.

"It's part of my plan," Celia stated. "Please trust me. Pour our coffee and leave. I want a private visit with Melissa. Don't forget to have the utilities turned on, open the dining room and have a blazing fire lit in all the fireplaces."

Sedwig bowed before Celia and quickly departed.

Celia turned to Melissa while she sipped her coffee.

"I wouldn't admit to anyone but you," Celia stated. Your mother and I were close; therefore, an explanation is in order. I saw you and your friend digging near the gazebo. Yes, that is the money I embezzled from the company and Larry often goes into the stash for expenditures. I also called the police when Leo and Nellie broke into the house. I was watching."

Celia stopped talking, then walked over to the side table and poured a refill "Would you like another?"

"No, thank you," Melissa answered in a weak shaky voice. She felt her knees buckle at the revelation.

Celia returned to the swivel chair and moved nervously back and forth as she drank.

"I'm not longer Celia. I've had paperwork and a passport issued in the name of Larry's new wife.

"I would like you to stay for the wedding," Celia pleaded. "It would mean so much to me."

"I guess I can postpone my trip for a few hours," Melissa agreed. She realized that Aunt Celia no longer existed, as before, and was the last living relative. Melissa had to come to terms with the shock.

"I would like to tell you more about your mother's earlier years. We were very close, your mother and I; I loved her dearly. I was also very jealous of her. When I brought your father home to meet our parents who would guess when he viewed your mother that was the end of my relationship with him. I was devastated but managed to carry on with the heartache. It went away shortly after I met Alfred. He was very rich and gave me everything I could ever desire. I did a very bad thing during your mother and father's courtship. I stole a diamond ring and locket from you mother's jewelry box. I want to give it to you. The locket contains two pictures: one side your mother and I: and the other a picture of your parents". Celia reached into the desk drawer and handed the two items to Melissa.

Melissa took the articles that Celia had stolen from her mother. Celia wasn't at all like her mother. Tears formed in Melissa's eyes; however, she quickly brushed them away.

"Well, I guess everything is said. Good luck with the million I left you as your aunt," she said. She got up, from the chair, walked over to Melissa and gave her a big hug.

Melissa made her way slowly down the stairs trying to absorb everything that had happened. The downstairs lights were aglow, fireplaces lit and it was as if the whole mansion came to life again. Jesse and her family arrived busily working in the kitchen. Jesse's mother came out and started re-arranging furniture for the wedding ceremony.

Melissa went into the kitchen. Jesse moved close to Melissa and said in a low voice. "I wanted to tell you the whole story but our family needed the money to start the restaurant and Celia wanted to keep it a secret. I think she is making a mistake marrying Larry," Jesse moved away and went back to the kitchen duties.

So now the whole truth was out.

Sedwig was muttering to himself, "I'll never accept this situation."

Melissa escaped from the activities by selecting a book and going into the sunroom where beautiful flowers surrounded the area like a garden wonderland. She could hide, in the abyss of a novel, while drowning out reality. The sun, came through the solar panel, and shed sunlight upon the indoor garden, which added to the warmth of the room. She reclined and read a new mystery book and tried to block out the excitement coming from the front room.

The florist delivered a variety of flowers for the wedding, which included fresh roses, lavender and lilacs. The fragrances meld together and filled the rooms. A symbolic Venus Fly trap was added to the conglomeration.

The kitchen area was busy preparing refreshments. A special aroma of a gastric scent escaped from the kitchen.

Guest arrived congratulating Larry and anxious to meet his new bride. The pastor arrived and had to be seated before the ceremony began. His trembling hands clutched the marriage ceremony book.

Sedwig announced the wedding service would begin in five minutes; therefore, Melissa returned the novel to the library, half read, and followed him into the front room, where several chairs were placed systematically in a row. Most were occupied by members of the community. She took a back seat next to Sedwig. As the wedding vows were exchanged Sedwig shook his head in a negative way and bent over. He was in love with Celia and upset with the wedding. Melissa placed a comforting arm around his shoulders.

The pastor asked," If anyone objects to these wedding vows. Speak now."

Sedwig looked at Melissa but neither wanted to speak up. So the pastor continued.

He muttered some words as he glanced at the marriage ceremony book.

"I now pronounce you man and wife," he spoke loudly as the ceremony was concluded.

"Now that you are husband and wife" Pastor Stanley announced. "You may kiss the bride."

Larry kissed Sandy lightly on the lips. She was dressed in a white suit, which seemed to compliment Larry's expensive tux. They looked great together. Was the wedding planned to hide the truth?

The elderly pastor enjoyed some refreshment that had been provided to members, of the community, as they gathered around and socialized. The pastor sought out Melissa for conversation.

"It's great Larry found a decent wife. Can you believe the last one was a crook? Imagine stealing Celia's identity," the pastor remarked to Melissa.

Melissa nodded her head in agreement. She stuffed food in her mouth so her voice couldn't be heard. The pastor took offense, in her action, and moved on to another location where several well-wishes had gathered. Melissa didn't want to be part of the sham and wanted to leave as soon as possible.

Melissa walked over to the newly wed couple. "I have to leave but I wish you the best."

Melissa drove away from the mansion. It would be the last time she would see her aunt.

She would never look back at the experience. Perhaps it was a dream and not a reality? It was not until she reached Massachusetts that she was fully aware of her surroundings. She had visited Vera's parents one time; therefore, she had to locate their residence by memory. The house was not too far from the highway. Melissa veered off the interstate, onto a smaller road, where a row of houses stood on Adams Street. It was dusk as she swung into the driveway and as Vera indicated, a key was placed under the door mat. The suitcase felt heavy as she managed to carry it into the small framed house. She was all alone and started to cry. Tomorrow she would call Vera and tell her of a safe arrival.

Vera came home on the weekend with groceries. Melissa had lived off fast foods previous to Vera's arrival. She still had the check from Celia's estate but hadn't cashed it. So money was getting low.

"You need some of my famous spaghetti," Vera stated. "Why so sad?"

Melissa broke down and sobbed. She had held her sadness inside but now she had a friend to share the experience with so the disclosure, about her aunt, poured out between sobs.

The story seemed unbelievable. Vera stood stunned and not able to move. She couldn't even speak.

"Well, I guess you'll have to do your best to forget the whole incident. You don't even know it was your aunt. It's twisted," Vera commented. "It could be dangerous. I can't believe

Larry drugged your drink and took advantage of you. The whole thing is unbelievable!"

"It was my aunt. She told me things about my mother's earlier days that only a relative would know," Melissa replied. She had finally gained her composure. "She gave me some of my mother's belongings. I didn't have the nerve to tell her what Larry did to me."

"You don't suppose someday Jesse might reveal the truth about Larry to your aunt?"

Vera became silent and concentrated on preparing a salad to accompany the spaghetti and meatballs dinner. The salad was served first and extra care was given to home made dressing. The boiling water gave Vera a signal that it ready for the spaghetti to be added, sauce stirred and topped off with burgundy wine as an additive. Vera kept busy not knowing what to say. She poured two glasses of burgundy wine to accompany the meal. Garlic bread came hot from the oven. The girls were quiet as they ingested the meal.

"I feel a lot better," Melissa acknowledged after dinner. "I guess I'll keep the inheritance money and invest part of it. The other sum should pay for school."

"Good for you," Vera replied. "Leave this horrible experience behind. Don't tell anyone about Larry's attack on you. Look forward not backward. Now we will make a lot of money this season at the restaurant. I've checked and the apartment we rented last year is available the end of the month."

"I'll move into the apartment, as soon as possible, even if the restaurant doesn't open till the middle of next month. I don't want to impose on your parents by staying here," Melissa explained.

"They are coming back soon. I'll be through with my finals soon. I'll join you," Vera stated.

Melissa finally came to terms of what had happened at the mansion. She regained her composure and looked forward to a summer reunion with Mark. She now regarded her aunt as dead.

The same summer resort apartment was available so Melissa made arrangements to rent it for the season. She took walks along the beach and relaxed in the late spring sun.

Soon Vera would be finished with finals and would join her. The restaurant opened the middle of the month.

Mark was overjoyed when he saw Melissa. "I've thought of you constantly throughout the school year and now we are together." Mark put his arms around her and held her tightly. Melissa knew Vera would no longer watch over her but allow this romance to bloom. The reunion with Mark, at the resort, was spectacular.

Harry returned and moved in with Mark while they, waited for permanent job offers. They hoped it would be their last season at the restaurant: both graduated with degrees and were seeking careers. Half way through the summer Mark was offered a job with benefits. Melissa invested some of her inheritance, in his firm, and it was an immediate promotion for Mark. The firm regarded her as wealthy investor, which was a plus for their upcoming wedding. Mark presented her with a two carat diamond engagement ring and wanted to consummate their love. Although it wasn't her first sex experience Melissa had no recollection of the encounter with Larry. The past was not mentioned.

Only the new jewelry box with Melissa's mother's diamond ring and locket was worth remembering. The other memories were blocked from her mind.

Vera and Melissa returned to college and managed to remain roommates through another scholastic year. This would be Vera's final college year. After graduation she planned to get a job, at the school where Harry taught disabled children. They would live together and hopefully a future commitment was in the offing.

Vera stayed in touch with John, the cook from the resort; therefore, he would send her newspapers from Maine to maintain contact. One article, in particular, caught Vera's interest. It was about an incident, which occurred at Station Harbor so Vera read the article out loud.

"A person fell overboard after a drinking party on the Yacht Merriment. A search and rescue was conducted and a body recovered. It was identified as Larry Sanderson. It seems as though, his widow, will inherit his property and an undisclosed amount of life insurance money.

"It sounds like Aunt Celia strikes again. Larry really deserved it." Melissa smirked.

"I wonder if she found out about his extra curricular activities," Vera answered.

"I wouldn't be at all surprised," Melissa replied.

The girls laughed.